BRUTAL PURSUIT

A richly-woven murder mystery, full of twists

DIANE M DICKSON

Paperback published by The Book Folks

London, 2019

Mass market edition (2)

ISBN 978-1-80462-290-2

www.thebookfolks.com

For Angela and Richard.

Prologue

When menacing clouds rolled across the open fields from Elsfield towards the Oxford Links Golf Club, Peter Baker wanted to abandon the game. Spencer Cartwright wasn't that bothered. He was losing. Again.

As the first great spots of rain peppered the sand in the bunkers, they knew there wouldn't be time to get back to the clubhouse safely. Already, the crash and roil of thunder was simultaneous with the lightning. Lights had flicked on in the blocks of flats near to the car park. The wind was up, trees whipped and swayed, leaves danced and raced across the greens. Suddenly it was wild.

They made a run for the nearest shelter. A small wooden building, out at the edge of the course; just on the border of the tree line. They could have huddled in the lee of the place, or under the small overhang of the roof, but the nearby trees were a danger. They had heard stories of electricity travelling along the ground, leaping from tree to man. It didn't matter whether this stuff was true or urban myth, it was enough to drive them to find better cover.

If they hadn't been so sensible, they could have avoided the image that would torment their dreams. The smell that stuck in the back of their throats. Spencer may even have avoided the heart attack, never fully recovering from the horror. But as for the rest of it, the wheel was already in motion.

A hasp and staple fastener, secured with a padlock, was easy to pry away from the thin wood. There was little damage, and they would pay the secretary. Not a problem.

The stench inside was thick; cloying. A sheet of some sort was thrown down over a heap in the corner. It was stained with patches, black fading to dark red at the borders. Flies swarmed around and over it. They coated the walls in a seething mass – crawled and hovered in a layer across the ceiling. The two men batted and swatted at the insects which had been panicked by the change of light and air.

Peter staggered back against the wooden wall and cried out in anguish as Spencer pulled back the dirty cloth. He knew already what was there; had known from the first whiff of putrefaction, from the shape of it, and from some inbuilt sixth sense.

As the full horror was revealed Peter slid inelegantly to the floor and Spencer vomited copiously, lunchtime salmon and pinot noir blighting the crime scene as it splashed and spread around his feet and across the corpse.

The body was naked and obviously male. It lay on its side, the knees bent upwards towards the chest, arms tucked in at the sides. The feet were bare, the hands were not there. The neck ended in a bloody stump.

Spencer looked around, searching for the head – he could never say why. His seething brain just couldn't accept that it was missing.

Chapter 1

Tanya Miller threw herself down onto the sofa in her living room and blew out a sigh. Sundays used to be okay. When she wasn't on duty, she would have a slow morning. She would have coffee and read the papers in bed, and then breakfast out in the little garden. If it rained, she would sit at her table in the window space. There would follow either a work-out or a jog, depending on her mood and then, after a long shower she would open a bottle of wine at lunchtime, just pouring one glass and saving the rest for later. She often caught up with paperwork in the afternoon, but in the quiet of her house, clean and calm, it was okay. Weekend or not she enjoyed being on top of the work, she had to be in control of that part of her life.

That was then.

She glanced around the room. There were several chargers on the coffee table, the cables in tangles, cascading onto the floor. A coffee mug sat on the wooden mantlepiece, and there was a puffa jacket discarded in the corner. From upstairs came the thump, thump, thump of music, tuneless and annoying and the whole house smelled of curry flavour Pot Noodle. She closed her eyes and laid her head against the settee back. *What the hell was she going to do about Serena?*

At the end of the last case, she had been sad when Charlie Lambert, closest thing to a friend that she had ever had, finally left for his new job in Merseyside. The sadness had been tempered by the thought that she would have her space back exclusively. Charlie had been a perfect guest – quiet, tidy, and a good cook. But now, he had gone to join his wife and baby who had moved ahead of him to their new house in Liverpool. The relief had been short-lived when Serena, Tanya's niece, had turned up at the door.

"I can't live at home anymore," she had sobbed. "Dad has gone off with his secretary and Mum isn't speaking to me."

There had been no choice but to take the girl in. She was damaged and fragile, recovering from being abducted and raped in Amsterdam, but Tanya had assumed it would be a couple of days, and then she could ship her off back to Fiona in Edinburgh. The marriage problems would be sorted, Serena would go into therapy or whatever and Tanya could once again ignore her relatives – apart from the odd card and present, sent out of an ever-diminishing sense of duty.

That was a month ago. Since then there had been visits from Fiona, along with the other two children, which had been chaotic and exhausting. There had been tearful discussions, pleading and shouting, endless phone calls and face time and at the end of it all, Serena was still in the spare bedroom. Now, life was all about catching up on laundry, sorting out healthy meals; and there was a constant dull battle about keeping the place clean.

Serena was used to having a cleaner tidying up after her constantly. Though Tanya did have Mrs Green once a week, it was no longer enough with a careless teenager, often left alone in the house. The girl was privileged and spoiled and didn't understand the concept of clearing up after herself or helping to do the cooking and washing.

Tanya was frustrated and more and more angry about the whole thing. But, when she rescued her from captivity, she had told the girl that she would be there for her. It had been a promise made in the emotion of the moment and she never really thought it would come to this. True, there was the money. It complicated things. With Tanya's finances in a mess, the contribution from her sister was a real help. But really it was not enough to make up for the chaos that her home life was becoming.

She drew in a breath. It had to be dealt with. Serena needed to return to some sort of normality – go back to college, back to Edinburgh and her mother. Tanya went to the kitchen, poured herself a glass of wine, a glass of cranberry juice for the girl, and walked out into the hallway. As her foot hit the first stair the phone on the little table chimed, vibrating across the polished surface.

"Miller."

"Control here, Detective Inspector, details are being forwarded by email about the discovery of a body at the Oxford Links Golf Club. Location details and co-ordinates for your sat nav have been sent. Please attend. The scenes of crime officers have been mobilised and the medical examiner is on route."

"Who pronounced death?" Tanya asked.

"Apparently, there was a GP in the clubhouse, but from what we hear there wasn't much doubt."

Tanya raised her eyebrows at the cryptic comment.

She felt the pounding of classic rock through the ceiling. Maybe a crime scene would be more peaceful than her own home at the moment. What a terrible thought.

"Thanks. I'll be on my way in the next few minutes."

She put the wine in the fridge and delivered the soft drink to Serena who was stretched out on the bed in the guest room, painting her nails.

"I have to go into work, Serena. I don't know how long I'll be. Don't go anywhere without letting me know and don't let anyone in – there is nobody expected. Oh, and

Serena, when I get back, we need to have a talk. We need to sort you out, okay?"

"Cool."

The girl didn't even bother to look up.

Chapter 2

It took around a half an hour on the quiet Sunday roads to reach the clubhouse. Tanya pulled into the tarmacked car park alongside an ugly block of flats. She stormed over to the uniformed officer on duty, flashed her warrant card and pointed towards the gateway. "Why is there no tape across the entrance, constable?"

"Sorry, ma'am, I was just told to log people in and out."

"And how do you intend to do that when the entrance is wide open? How are you going to stop them?"

The young policeman lowered his head and lifted his clipboard to wave it between them. "Most of the members are still inside, only a couple have left."

"And where do you imagine they are now?"

"Sorry, ma'am, I don't know what you mean," he said.

"Of the people who have left, where are they? There has been a body found and you have allowed people to drive away. Tell me, constable, does that seem sensible?"

She was raging and struggling not to lose her temper. These days it was a nightmare justifying a dressing down and the easiest thing was to hold the passion in check.

Again, he waved his clipboard at her. "I have their names and addresses, ma'am."

There was no point to this, she could see that, and it was wasting time. "Put some tape across the entrance, constable. Don't let anyone else leave until I tell you it's okay, and don't let anyone else in. Do, however, get the details of anyone trying to gain access. Is that clear?"

"Yes, ma'am; thank you, ma'am. Er…"

"Problem?"

"Well, I haven't been given any tape. I think it's with the SOCO team down by the hut. My mate took the squad car down there."

Tanya pointed to his radio and raised her eyebrows. He blushed a furious red.

"Sort it would you, constable?"

"Yes, ma'am."

According to the email, the body was in a small hut hidden by a stand of trees on the east side of the course. Already someone had marked out a safe route. Making sure to stay on the designated path, she stomped across the grass which had been soaked by the recent storm and then towards the first green. Here at least there had been some professional activity. Blue and white tape snapped in the wind. The medical examiner's car was pulled onto the verge and the SOCO van stood alongside, the rear doors open.

Another uniformed constable was on duty, but this one held up his hand as she approached. She flashed her ID and he noted her name on his chart. "Suit up please, ma'am," he said.

In the back of the van was a box containing suits, masks, and overshoes – Tanya helped herself. There was activity behind the trees, and she felt the familiar frisson of excitement that always shamed her a little when attending a crime scene. It wasn't that she was unsympathetic to the victims, but this was what she lived for. The responsibility to seek out evil and extract some sort of justice for those who had come to harm. It was too late for most of them, but it was the only option left.

There was no plastic tent. Instead, there was a folding pergola with white walls erected around the doorway to the small wooden building. As she approached, she heard Simon Hewitt issuing instructions. She felt a little flutter in her chest. She still wasn't sure he wanted their relationship to be more than professional. However, that was what other people had told her and the idea was enough to make her awkward in his company. It wouldn't do. She took a steadying breath and stepped into the reeking, fly-blown interior of the crime scene.

Chapter 3

They had set up floodlights, and behind the low hum of conversation she heard a generator rumbling amongst the trees. The hut was dirty, flies buzzed back and forth, bouncing off the lights, and she could see from the mass of black bodies on the floor that there had been more, many more. The smell was bad, and Tanya breathed through her mouth. The mask sucked inward with each inhalation. It was vile. She closed her mind to it and concentrated on her survey of the scene.

Narrow shelves lining the walls were stacked with supplies, bottles and jerry cans. There were tools stored in a corner. The interior was draped with spider webs, and there was dust everywhere. It didn't look as though the place was used regularly.

Tanya picked out the senior scenes of crime officer. "Dave, what have we got?"

"A bloody mess in more ways than one, Detective Inspector. As you see we're going to have lots of evidence from the victim, except his head, which appears to have taken itself off somewhere. The hands are missing, which is not – well, not that handy?"

It was corny and cringeworthy, but Dave Chance was known for his terrible humour and she understood. As with most first responders, it helped to get him through the awful things he dealt with. She didn't laugh, and he hadn't expected her to. His blue eyes sparkled behind the mask and the skin around them crinkled as he smiled at her, then he looked away, glancing around the small space.

"It's going to take a while. We'll need to do a fingertip search here and outside, although, with the recent storm, that won't throw up much I shouldn't think. The rain has probably obliterated whatever was there. In here, well I don't hold out much hope for fingerprints, not with this rough wood and, as you can see, it's all pretty dirty and dusty. The floor's been swept a bit, just a movement of the dust really but it means there's no chance of footprints. Maybe there were some and that's why they cleaned it. I'm waiting to hear what Dr Hewitt has to say about the body. If the bloke was killed here, there might be something more than just his own trace evidence, but I rather imagine we're going to be told he's been dumped as we see him now, and that does us no favours. Oh, but we do have this."

He bent down and extracted an evidence bag from a plastic box on the floor. Inside was a small but hefty looking padlock. "This was attached to the hasp and staple." He pointed at another bag still in the plastic container. "The blokes who made the discovery levered it off to gain access. So, whoever left our friend here must have handled this. We've dusted it for prints, but that was a nonstarter, no surprise there. If we can find the key though – ta-da!" He described a flourish with his other hand. "That would unlock the whole case." He rocked his head from side to side, the muscles of his face lifting in another grin.

"Ha ha. Funny – not." Tanya shook her head at him. "Thanks, Dave, if anything unexpected comes up let me know, will you?"

"Course I will. This yours now, is it?"

"I have to see the DCI, but they sent me, so, I'm hopeful."

"So, you're all better then?" He had replaced the lock into his evidence box and now pointed at her arm, which had needed surgery after the violent events at the end of her last case.

"Yes, it's fine thanks. I've done my physio like a good girl, and they've signed me off and put me back on the rota."

"Ah, just in time for this, lucky you."

"I guess so. I'll go and have a word with Dr Hewitt, and then I've got stuff to sort. Thanks, Dave."

"No problem. It's good to have you back in harness. Is the enquiry about your last job finished?" he asked.

"Yes, thank goodness. The DCI always told me there was nothing for me to worry about, but it was a big relief when they said we'd done it all right."

"Course you did. You always do."

She didn't make friends easily and his comments surprised her. With Charlie gone maybe it would be nice to have some other, different mates among her colleagues after all. More than that though, she appreciated the unasked-for vote of confidence. As for friends, trouble was she wasn't sure she really wanted any. Life was simpler without them.

Chapter 4

There was no way to cross the dirty, fly strewn floor without disturbing the small evidence tents that the SOCO team had placed to protect things that needed to be examined more closely, or where samples had been taken. There were already several people stepping carefully around each other.

The pale shape of the naked man was tight against the wall, the cover a stained and noisome heap alongside. The place stank of vomit, but she had already been told that the scene was contaminated by the reaction of one of the poor individuals who had found this carnage. The medical examiner was speaking quietly into his recorder, while his assistant and a photographer made notes and recorded the terrible images. Simon turned and raised a hand. Tanya indicated that she would wait outside. He nodded and continued his examination of the corpse.

She stepped into the plastic porch and phoned her boss. "I'm at the golf course, sir. There's no doubt it's a suspicious death. Parts of the body are missing."

"Are you fit, Tanya?"

"I am. I was signed off last week. I'm itching to get back to work. I've been stuck at home with paperwork and my niece for weeks. I'm tearing my hair out."

He laughed. "I can imagine. Okay. Get your usual team together, those who are available. I'll make some calls from here, clear their assignments. Let me know if you need anything else. You're going to be one short anyway, now that Charlie has gone. I'll see what I can do, maybe find you another bod. Keep me informed and I'll see you in the morning for an update. Call my secretary to set up a time."

"Yes, sir, thank you." She smiled, then felt guilty – pleasure was inappropriate, but it felt so good to be working again.

Her first call was to Kate Lewis. The Detective Constable had been assigned, with several others, to investigate a spate of violent muggings. The victims were mostly old people who didn't understand what had happened to them or why. It was depressing and ugly, she was happy to move on.

"Thanks, ma'am. Do you want me to make the other calls, save you time? I can go in now if you like and sort a room for us, have the computer generate an operational name. It's early yet and it'll save time in the morning."

"Brilliant, thanks, Kate. I'm looking forward to seeing you again. It's being cleared with your current DI. Will they be able to manage? Without you?"

"I reckon so, they are about ready to bring in the scum. It's winding up."

"Excellent. I'll call Sergeant Harris myself. I need him to come out here and meet me."

She liked Kate. They had forged a good working relationship. Though she would never understand the older woman's lack of ambition, she had great respect for her skills on the computer and her ability to spot things hidden in the data. She could leave it to Kate to have things ready to go by the time they met up in the morning.

There was still no sign of Simon Hewitt, so she called Serena at home. "I'm going to be a while yet. Can you sort yourself something to eat?"

"Yeah. I might go out anyway." The girl sounded sullen and bad-tempered.

"No, I don't want you to. You need to stay in. We discussed this, Serena. I told you that if you were going to stay with me it was by my rules. I don't know how long I'll be, and I don't want to be worrying about you on top of everything else. Stay in."

"Oh, bloody hell."

With the expletive, the girl cut the call. This wasn't going to work for much longer. It had been manageable while she had been on sick leave. They had spent hours together, talking. Tanya had let the girl unburden herself, not only about the events in Holland but the problems at home that had led to her rebellion. There had been some laughs, a few trips to the cinema and Pizza Hut. Now, she would have no time for dealing with a moody and temperamental teen. She called her sister and was relieved to hear the voice mail message.

"Fiona, we need to talk. I'm back in work now, things are going to have to change. I can't deal with my job *and* your daughter. Ring me. Leave it until later, after nine."

She knew she sounded sharp, but this wasn't her problem. When Serena had disappeared, a few months earlier, Tanya had gone to Scotland and found her. Though she had very possibly saved her life, she didn't believe that made her responsible for her ongoing care. It was time for Fiona to step up and take responsibility. She had always been spoiled and selfish but enough was enough. The poor soul inside this stinking hut deserved all of her attention, and he would have it.

The plastic curtain over the doorway moved and she turned to see Simon Hewitt stepping through. He pulled down his face mask. "Tanya, lovely to see you again. You look well, but actually a bit, erm, irritated. Is there something wrong?"

She laughed. "Well yes, but I'm handling it. It's good to see you again Dr… Simon."

It was. He looked good, in spite of the unflattering outfit.

He held out a hand. "Welcome back."

Chapter 5

Tanya phoned Paul Harris as she trudged back along the designated route towards the car park and the little huddle of brick buildings. "Sorry to interrupt your weekend, Sergeant."

"That's okay, ma'am. The wife's got her family here, it'll be a relief to escape to be honest. I reckon I'll be there in about half an hour, give or take a bit for the traffic."

"There's a plod on duty, I'll let him know where I am so that you can find me," Tanya said.

In the clubhouse people were doing their best to look appalled and sad, but they couldn't hide their ghoulish, suppressed excitement. All eyes turned to the door as Tanya walked through. She glared at the nearest person – a red-faced, overweight individual in a check sweater and pink trousers. "Where will I find whoever is in charge?"

The man obviously thought he was deserving of a bit more deference, he'd paid his dues after all; greens fees, membership – this was his club. "Who are you exactly?"

Tanya didn't speak, she flashed her warrant card and stared silently at him across the small space. Tension built, but at the end of the day, she was 'the authorities' and had the upper hand. With a huff, he waved towards a door set in an alcove beside the bar. He wasn't giving up without a fight though. "When will I be able to leave? I have things to do; we all have things to do."

Tanya had begun to walk away but she stopped and turned. For a moment she lowered her head. When she raised her eyes to him, he took a step back at the glint of anger sparking there. "I will let you know when you can leave. We will have to speak to you – all of you."

She glanced back and forth to include the others in the room – some sixteen or seventeen people; nearly all men. "You will need to give us your contact details, amongst other things. We can't get on with that until I have more officers available, so I ask you to be patient. Have another drink maybe. This is a serious situation and there are routines we will follow. Now, excuse me."

As she moved away the antagonist huffed under his breath. "I'll have a word about this, the Assistant Chief Constable is a personal friend."

Tanya half turned towards him. "In that case, sir, I am sure he'll be pleased to hear that everyone co-operated fully with our enquiries."

She threaded her way through the groups of golfers and knocked on the office door. It was flung open and the secretary stepped aside, allowing her through. He peered at the members muttering in the club room, and wagged a hand at them, as if to say – *go away, stop milling around.* Then he turned to follow Tanya. Once inside, with the door firmly closed on the frustrated, nosey group outside, he indicated a chair in front of his desk and he passed behind it to take his own seat.

"Were they giving you hassle? I'm sorry. Everyone is upset, stressed out. It's terrible – Spencer and Peter are dreadfully distressed. I wonder if they should be taken to the hospital, to be honest. I've put them in the first aid room, I hope that was okay. They weren't fit to be out there, with everyone asking them about it. Was that okay?"

"Is there anyone with them?"

"There was Dr Lawler, but he's had to go to an emergency. There's a police constable, one of the ones who arrived first, and the club first aider."

"Excellent. I'll go and speak to them now. I have my sergeant on the way and, as soon as we can, we'll take statements from your members and let them get off home."

"Will the club have to close?"

At the question, Tanya's eyes widened in surprise. "You do understand there's a body out there?"

"Well yes, but I just thought maybe if we just close that tee, we could allow members to play. Not today, obviously; well, it's too late anyway, being wet with the storm and all." He glanced out of the window.

Tanya understood that people dealt with trauma in different ways but nonetheless she was appalled. "I'm sorry Mr…"

"Traynor, Stephen Traynor. Secretary."

"Right, well, Mr Traynor, your club will be closed until we're satisfied that we have found whatever there is to be found. By that I mean, anything and everything that may help us to identify this person and hopefully lead us to who did this dreadful thing. I don't know how long that might be."

He didn't have an answer. She saw him struggle; watched as he acknowledged he had screwed up.

He coughed. "Well, yes, of course, of course. I just… the thing is, you see they will want to know." He pointed at the door. "The owners, they'll be in touch no doubt, I just …" His speech fizzled out and he coughed again, dragged a notepad towards himself. "What is it you'd like us to do now? We'll be as much help as we can, obviously."

"Thank you. We'll do what we can to move things along swiftly. In the meantime, I would appreciate a room where myself and my sergeant can interview your members and the staff."

"You can use this one, for as long as you need. There's a phone here, there's WiFi; oh yes, I'll let you have the password."

Tanya was amused. Embarrassment and over-reaction made him gabble and become effusive. She nodded, glancing around.

"This will be fine. Thank you."

There was a quiet knock on the door. Traynor opened it and Paul Harris stepped in. He grinned at her. Although he wasn't her favourite member of the team, a misogynist and at times crude, she smiled back at him.

This was happening, she was back.

She walked across the little room, passed the shelves of trophies and a golf trolley with a bag of clubs on it pushed up against the wall.

She spoke quietly, just above a whisper. "Paul, good to see you. We can use this room to interview the people outside. I don't think we need much beyond the basics at this stage. Names and addresses and what have you. We can probably get through it ourselves in an hour or so unless something unexpected comes up."

She glanced at her phone, "I'm still waiting to speak to Dr Hewitt, but I have a feeling the death occurred a while ago, probably not here, so it is very likely the golfers who were on the course today will be of little help. We do need a list of all the members and when they were here last. I noticed there is CCTV on the car park, possibly elsewhere. We'll need to have the recording from that for as far back as possible, and at least for the past week. I'll speak to the secretary about that myself." She jerked her head backwards indicating the man sitting at the desk, craning his ears for any snippet that would give him one up on the other members.

"Right, boss, do you want me to go down and view the deceased?" Harris said.

"No need, and to be honest you wouldn't want to. Could you ask that numpty outside to let Dr Hewitt know where I am? I would like a word before he leaves. He can radio his rather more intelligent mate who is down at the scene. Then you come back here. The sooner we get started, the sooner these people can get off home."

"On it, boss."

As he left, she turned to find the secretary clearing things from the top of his desk. "Thank you, Mr Traynor. If you could just show me where the first aid room is, and then maybe you'd like to wait in the bar with the members."

Chapter 6

There was no doubt the two men who had discovered the body were shocked and distressed. Unless they were brilliant actors, their reaction to the grisly find negated any possibility that they could have been involved. Indeed, once she had the complete account, Tanya dismissed them as nothing other than unfortunate witnesses. Anyone who had dumped the body in that hut would never go back to seek shelter there, not even during the greatest storm in Christendom.

"Do you think either of you need to be taken to the hospital, and treated for shock or whatever? We could take you in a patrol car, no need for an ambulance."

They both declined, and Peter Baker raised his shot glass and wiggled it back and forth. "A drop of brandy helped, rare to get a freebie around here." He managed a short humourless laugh. "My wife's agreed to come and take us both home. I don't think I'm fit to drive and Spencer's not."

He nodded towards his friend who was sat, head down, with his shaking hands clasped between his thighs. Apart from answering direct questions, he hadn't spoken. His grey eyes had flooded with tears as he described the dreadful scene.

He gulped and spoke quietly. "I don't think either of us will ever get that out of our minds, Detective. I can still smell it. How can you get rid of that? It's in my throat. God, I swear I can taste it."

"If you smear something else just under your nose it sometimes helps – something like Vicks, that sort of thing."

"Thank you, thanks. I'll do that when I get home. Can we go?"

"Yes. We may need to speak to you again but thank you for your help. I'm sorry you've had to go through this."

As he stood and picked up his coat, Cartwright turned to her again. "I don't suppose you know who he is – that poor bugger?"

"Not yet, sir, but we will find out. We'll find who did this and we'll bring them to justice. It's what we do."

He lifted his coat and held it inches from his face. "I can smell it on here." He thrust it towards the first aid man. "Jamie, do me a favour would you? Burn this."

They trudged out through the silent bar room, all eyes turned towards them, but they kept their gaze down and didn't acknowledge anyone. A car pulled to a halt in the middle of the car park and a tall, slender woman jumped out. She gave Peter Baker a quick hug and then leaned to give Cartwright an air kiss near each cheek before opening doors for both of them. Tanya wondered if they would ever fully recover. Doing the job, you became more accustomed to the horrible things you saw, but as she watched them drive away, she lifted her arm and sniffed at the sleeve of her own jacket. It was there, maybe in her nose, maybe on her clothes – despite the protective suit.

It didn't take them long to interview the rest of the members. Some had been out on the course and scurried for cover when they saw the storm coming. Some had been in the clubhouse waiting for it to pass. Several were there only for the drinks and the break from Sunday chores, and relatives, and shopping with their wives. There was nothing concrete to ask them yet, all that was required was to record their names and addresses and get a feel for them. Nothing stood out, nobody appeared particularly nervous, nobody was flustered or evasive. It was just as she had expected it to be.

Simon Hewitt walked into the bar just as the last of them drove off. The constable on duty replaced the crime scene tape, glancing back as he did so to see Tanya watching. She smiled to herself – it hadn't been his best day and she could imagine him yearning for the end of his shift.

"Tanya." The medical examiner held out a hand. He had removed the protective suit and was dressed in well-worn jeans, a sweatshirt, and a fur-lined leather jacket. Down time clothes. "It's good to see you looking so well. Injury all healed now?"

In response, she flexed and bent her arm. "Good as new. The pin will stay in forever apparently, but there's no pain now and I have full movement."

"So, you're back in the swing then?"

"I'm getting there. I have to admit I was bored to death at the house. Serena is still there but it's like living with an alien. I think it's been good for her but it's time to finish it. She needs to go home, so this is great."

She felt her cheeks heat as she realised what she'd said. "Well, not great, obviously for that bloke." She pointed back towards the hut. "Not good for him, bu… oh, you know what I mean."

Simon was nodding at her. "It's alright, I know what you mean. Anyway, the victim. I expect you saw there was no head. The hands are missing. They've been hacked off – violently and inexpertly – possibly with something heavy and sharp: a machete, an axe, that sort of thing. But not here. There would have been blood everywhere, bone fragments – all manner of evidence. No, he was brought here, the parts of him that we have at any rate. Apart from that, there isn't all that much I can tell you until I have a proper look, back at the morgue. He's been dead a few days, I'll be able to be more precise when I've examined the development of insect larvae and so on. I'll be able to get to him in the morning, I hope. I'll start early. Will you come down?"

"Yes, I will," Tanya said.

"About seven then. The reception staff won't be there. I'll buzz you in if you text when you reach the car park."

He shook her hand again. "Welcome back, Detective Inspector, we've missed you."

Again, she felt herself blush. *Stop it, he's just being nice.*

He walked out of the car park, along the safe route towards his car.

There was nothing else to be done there. The fingertip search would be postponed until the morning. It was dark, and wet, and cold; nothing to see. The SOCO team would continue their work in the hut. Once the body was moved, which would hopefully be in the next few hours, they too would leave. This wasn't where the murder had taken place and although there would be evidence it wouldn't tell them much. They needed to find the original site. That would be a major challenge.

The recordings from the CCTV were being downloaded onto flash drives. She left Paul Harris waiting for them while she drove home through a wet and windy night. She would have a shower, a glass of wine and then start her notes – ready to speak to her team early in the morning.

The house was in darkness, so the chaos in the kitchen was all the more shocking, revealed as it was in the sudden glare as she turned on the lights.

Chapter 7

Tanya thundered up the stairs, thumped once on the door of the guestroom, and threw it open. She flicked on the overhead light and stormed across the littered floor to the bed where Serena was pushing herself up against the pillows, hands shielding her eyes from the sudden brightness.

"Aunty Tan," she muttered. "What the hell?"

"Get up. Come on, get up," Tanya said. "Get out of bed and come downstairs."

"Oh shit. Look I'll clean it up in the morning, I promise." Serena licked her dry lips and reached for the bottle of water standing on the bedside table. "Oh God. My head's splitting, I can't do this now." She turned away and began to slide down back under the duvet.

"Oh no! No, you don't!"

Tanya grabbed the corner of the covers and pulled them to the floor. "Get up now. Go downstairs and clean up that mess in the kitchen. Then you and me are having words. How dare you? How dare you take my drink, my food without permission, and leave my home in that state? How dare you? You spoiled, ungrateful sod."

"I was bored, I had some friends over. What? Did you expect me to give them water to drink, no snacks? Anyway, it wasn't all your food, they brought pizza with them. We just had some beers, some wine. Chill, yeah. It's cool. I'll replace it, I'll order some online tomorrow. No problem. Your cleaner can come in an extra day, I'll pay her."

Tanya was furious. She looked down at the teenager and felt absolute disgust. How could it be that Fiona, who had grown up in a house where every penny was counted, had raised such a thoughtless, self-entitled child? But of course, Fiona herself had been the selfish, demanding sister. She was the one for whom the money was somehow always found to fulfil her wants and desires. So, this was the result.

Tanya had thought that Serena was grateful to be there; that she appreciated her aunt sacrificing her precious privacy. How could that be when she had trashed the kitchen, helped herself to wine from the rack and then walked away expecting someone else to clean up after her?

"I can't do this anymore, Serena. I know I said that I'd help you, support you, but this is no good. You'll have to go home. I'm back in work now. I have to be able to give everything to my job. I can't have this crap."

"Aunty Tan, you're getting this out of proportion. Okay, I'm sorry I made a mess. We were having a good time, that's all. I was on my own, rang a couple of friends and we had a laugh. I suppose I could have cleaned up but honestly, I was wasted. I didn't think you'd mind."

Tanya closed her eyes and shook her head as another thought pushed aside the fury. "Who were these people anyway? How come you have friends here? You've never lived in Oxford"

"Mates from Edinburgh, down here visiting the university. I met up with them the other day and then – well, I just rang them. Look, I really feel awful. Can we talk about this tomorrow?"

Tanya bit back the first response – swearing wouldn't help. Struggling with control she clenched her hands into fists. *Only fight the battles you can win.* She knew that was a good rule to live by, and she had work to do, important work. Tomorrow though, tomorrow this girl was going to scrub the kitchen end to end, pay for the wine that she had drunk and then, if Fiona didn't get it sorted, Tanya herself was going to arrange travel for Serena back to Scotland.

Chapter 8

Tanya was deeply asleep. She had worked late, organising her plans, starting the murder book – albeit on her laptop – with locations, images and the names and contact details of everyone they had interviewed. She knew that Kate would already have all of this, but needed her own copy, arranged in her own way.

It was just becoming dawn, grey light brightening the window blind, when her phone began to vibrate across the top of the bedside cabinet, startling her awake. She grabbed the handset and held it in front of her face. Simon Hewitt's ID filled the screen. She coughed. "Dr Hewitt, good morning."

"Good morning, Detective Inspector. Sorry it's so early. I told control that I would ring you myself to save time."

"Right, I didn't realise…" Tanya turned the alarm clock towards her. It was six thirty. "I thought you said seven. Sorry, I won't be long. I'll be with you soon as I can," she said.

"It's okay. I'm not calling from the morgue. I'm out in the cold, wet morning." He laughed quietly. "It seems that we may have found our head."

"Head?" In her befuddled state, she struggled to catch up with the conversation.

"Yes, a fisherman out at Duke's Cut. Do you know it?"

"No, I don't think so." She twisted out from under the covers and squirmed out of her T-shirt. Dragging it over her shoulders, she passed the phone from hand to hand through the sleeves, hoping he couldn't hear the rustle of fabric.

"It's a fishing lake, not all that far from the golf club. I'm there now. This poor angler came out looking for some bream or roach and bagged himself a sack full of body parts instead. I was called because of yesterday. I thought you'd want to have a look before we move it."

"Thanks, yes. Thank you. I'll be with you as quickly as I can."

She clicked off the phone, dragged on her jeans and sweater, and ran through to the loo. She dashed down the stairs and fished her boots out from under the hall chair. She turned towards the kitchen and was hit full in the face by the mess.

She tore a page from the shopping pad and scrawled across it in black marker. 'Clean this up, Serena. I'll call you later. Don't go out.' That done she grabbed her jacket, car keys and sat nav, and slammed the door behind her.

She had Kate on speed dial. Once she'd set up the hands-free, she gave her a quick rundown of the situation. "I need you to arrange for divers. They should meet me out at the lake. Call Detective Chief Inspector Scunthorpe, he'll have to approve the expenditure. What time are the team coming in?"

"In at eight and briefing at half past nine. I was allowing time for you to attend the post-mortem examination," Kate said.

"Right – well that's going to be delayed now, I guess. Look, I'll ring you from the lake."

"Yes, ma'am. Oh, we've got a name – Operation Rambler."

"Noted. Thanks, I'll see you in a couple of hours."

She set the sat nav, pulled into the main road and with a quick glance in the rear-view mirror at her little house, the light still burning in the bedroom window, she left the problems of Serena and her friends behind.

Chapter 9

The drizzling rain had become a downpour by the time she arrived at Duke's Cut. Tanya flashed her ID at the officer stationed in front of the dilapidated metal gate. He noted her name on his form. "Park at the end of this road, Ma'am, you'll see the others."

Splashing and jolting down a narrow track, she joined the conglomeration of official vehicles sitting in the puddled mud of the small car park. She changed into her wellingtons, which were always in the car boot these days. Too many pairs of ruined shoes and wet feet had taught her valuable lessons. Once she had dragged on protective gear, and the disposable booties onto her feet, she grabbed her little recorder and went to see what horror was waiting in this quiet, picturesque spot.

The usual controlled hubbub was subdued by drenching rain. It was turning into a very wet month and it was really the last thing they needed. Uniformed constables skulked under trees waiting for the inevitable instructions that would see them trudging through muck and mud in a search which would more than likely turn up nothing. The big find had already happened, but the uncomfortable drudgery that was part and parcel of the job would still need to be done. She acknowledged them as she passed and received a few desultory nods in response.

The white suits of the scene of crime investigators, moving between the vans and the centre of attention, were turned just a little translucent by the rain. Already water was dripping into Tanya's eyes from the tendrils of hair poking out from under the edge of the hood. She raised a hand and tucked the sopping strands more neatly inside. The only people not cursing the weather were the little group of three divers unloading gear from the back of a van – they were already in wetsuits, and in their element. They had arrived very quickly. Again, she was impressed by Kate's efficiency.

The location of a blue plastic igloo drew Tanya towards the edge of the water. A few metres away a rod leaned against a tree where a dejected figure sat on top of a plastic box, his head lowered, elbows resting on his knees.

Inside the tent, Simon Hewitt, a photographer, and an assistant making notes, crouched in a small huddle around a dark shape that had been pulled onto the bank. Strands of slimy waterweed shone in the beam of floodlights, making the whole scene surreal and artificial looking. The fishing hook was still attached to the object and a length of line lay across the grass.

As Tanya joined the group around the sack, Simon Hewitt raised his head and nodded. Tanya gave a small wave and lowered herself onto her haunches.

"Poor chap over there opened the bag," Simon told her. He pointed towards the figure under the tree. "We haven't done much to it. Thought we'd wait for you to see it in location, though I'm not sure how much that will help. I see you arranged for an underwater team."

"Yes, I don't suppose there is much more for us to find now, but you never know. We don't have any weapon, yet," Tanya said.

"Well, we'll get on with this. Have you finished with your pictures?" Simon looked up at the photographer.

"Got everything I need, I reckon," she said. "I'll video this bit."

There wasn't much to see and what there was didn't look like anything human. The head, still partly obscured by wet canvas, was the palest white. Strands of dark hair were glued flat to the dome of the skull by water and slime. The fisherman had obviously realised quickly what his haul was and had stayed his hand once the neck of the sack exposed its grisly contents. Consequently, the opening was only rolled down to just above the brows. Tanya was glad. She would see it eventually, but later, in the clean surroundings of the autopsy suite. It wouldn't be so horrific then. She knew that the eyes would probably be gone by now. Even though the ghastly thing had been inside the bag, small creatures would have gained access and there was evidence that rats had given it their attention.

"It can't have been very far in." Tanya pointed to the small holes.

"No, apparently there is an area of shallow water just beyond the bank, where it's silted up. This must have been caught there just under the surface. If it had been thrown into the main lake it might never have surfaced. Perhaps whoever it was didn't know the area, or maybe they just didn't want to stray too far from the car park," Simon replied.

"Yes, it would be hard going in the dark. According to information Constable Lewis sent me while I was driving here, the place is quite popular in the daytime with fishermen, birdwatchers and what have you. Especially at the weekend. So, my thinking right now is that whoever disposed of this came at night. Thanks, Simon. Shall I see you back at the morgue?"

She paused and looked down at the heap on the ground. "I suppose this is our head? The chances of a head in one place and a completely different body so nearby are pretty remote, aren't they? Are the hands there?"

"Well, we'll get this back and then we can have a closer look and we'll know for sure." As he spoke, Simon nodded to the assistant who moved closer and unfolded a large evidence bag.

"From what I've been able to observe, there is more than just the head. Do you see?" Simon pointed with a gloved finger towards the bottom of the sack where the canvas bulged again. "There is something there, of course, I can't know for sure, but I think it's very possible."

He directed his next comment to the technician. "No need to worry too much about the area around it, the fisherman just dropped it there. Just the stuff from directly underneath in case anything has seeped or fallen from the sack."

He turned back to Tanya. "Give me another couple of hours and then I'll meet you back at my place."

"What time did you get the call?" she asked.

"An hour or so ago. I don't live far away, so we've been enjoying this lovely weather, haven't we?" He stood and now turned to address the others on the scene.

"Yeah, great start to the week," one of the women grumbled.

Simon laid a hand on her shoulder. "Oh well, Sandy, look at it this way, things can only improve." He handed a vial of samples to her.

She bent to place it in a plastic crate along with several others. "Yeah, and I've heard that before," she said.

Tanya left them and walked out into the rain to have a chat with the witness who was now pouring himself a hot drink from his thermos. The thought of coffee was enticing, and she wondered what the chances of him offering her a cup would be. In the event, he didn't.

Chapter 10

Ana sat on the steps of the caravan and lit a cigarette. The rain had ceased now, and although it was cold and damp, she would rather be outside. She glanced around and for a moment her eyes filled with tears. She brushed them aside impatiently. There was no point in tears, regret, sadness. No point at all. It had never made any difference. But now she was very lonely, she had another reason to cry.

From her perch in the little doorway, she could see, across the fields, the red-tiled roofs of houses. She had never been closer to them, but she could tell that they were large. In magazines, she had seen pictures of the houses in the UK. Gardens filled with roses, long driveways with shrubs and trees, garages containing shiny cars. Swimming pools, blue tiled, with clear water sparkling in the sunshine. Garden parties, barbecues. She had known that much of it was never going to be hers, but she had thought that some of it – maybe a small house, a little patch of green grass, a gate and a path – could have been hers.

She had been a fool.

She was still a fool, and now she was a lonely fool. She could have gone with the others; they had begged her to. She wondered where they were. Scotland or Wales maybe.

London. Probably they had gone to London. They might be standing right now looking at Buckingham Palace. She imagined Elian and his crooked grin; how he would love the soldiers and the horses. Dani was kinder than she was – if she had made a run for it, she wouldn't have taken the idiot with her – but she hoped they were okay, that they were having fun; both of them. She'd been too much of a coward, but Dani had shrugged the threats aside. "It's nothing. He will do nothing," she'd said.

Ana sniffed, stubbed out the cigarette and turned her head. From inside the nasty tin caravan, she could hear Emilia coughing. She needed medicine. When the man came, she would ask him again to bring medicine.

She clambered back into the dark little space and began to straighten and tidy her bed. She wondered how long it would be before another woman arrived to occupy what had been Dani's. Maybe never, maybe they could have this extra space. It was a little luxury, just her and Emi. The other woman was under the covers. Ana poured a cup of coffee, holding it out to her. "You need to get up, it's time to go to work. The man will be here soon. He'll be mad if we make him wait. You'll feel better when you get up. You'll be better when you have something to do. Come on."

The other woman took the cup, nodded her thanks, but lost herself in another paroxysm of coughing. She looked pale and sick. Maybe they would let her stay in bed today. Maybe she would die, maybe it would be better for her if she did. Death could solve so many problems. Ana turned away and pulled some jeans and a shirt from the pile of clothes on the floor. *What was she, Emi's mother?* The woman was old enough to look after herself. She had children back at home; she knew about illness.

Dragging on a nylon jacket, she poured the last of the coffee into a mug and went outside to wait for the man. She also was better when there was something to do.

Something to fill the spaces in her mind that otherwise let in the sadness and the anger.

When the dirty van pulled up, she could hear that the others were already inside, mumbling and clearing their throats, shuffling on the floor. The driver pulled open the sliding door and stood back to let her clamber in. The men shuffled closer together. There was an early morning stink of dirty clothes and bad breath, farts, and body odour. She breathed through her mouth. Emi dragged herself inside and lowered slowly to the floor and the door slid shut with a rattle.

Chapter 11

The witness didn't add much to what Tanya had already been told. Robert, 'call me, Bob' Peters, had cast his line and been surprised to have a bite so quickly. Immediately he started reeling it in, he'd known it was not a fish.

"People throw rubbish in," he said, "I just thought it was a bag of rags or something, maybe some drowned puppies."

He was surprisingly calm, but two tours of duty in Helmand Province and his current work with the traffic officers, scraping bodies off the motorway, accounted for that. He admitted that he had been shocked at first but, no, he didn't need counselling, or accompanying home.

"Is there anything else you can think of that seemed odd to you? Did you see any other cars, anything at all?" Tanya asked.

"No, just the bag and I didn't look at that very closely. I've seen enough of that sort of stuff." He gave her a wry smile. "I suppose my fishing's over for today then, eh?"

She nodded. "Yes, I'm afraid so. Thank you for your assistance."

She handed over a card with her name and rank. "If you need any help in the future – from the victim support services, for instance – or if you remember anything else, just give me a ring."

She addressed the uniformed officers briefly and left them in the care of a grizzled old sergeant who had seen this sort of thing before. He had them stepping out into the rain, wearing what he described as 'bloody silly babygrows' but with clear and explicit instructions which left her in no doubt that, in the unlikely event there was anything to find, his team would find it.

The underwater guys were ready to enter the lake.

"We haven't found any sort of weapon yet," she told them. "We still don't know for certain whether this is the head to match our body, but it seems that it's likely. Heavy knives, saws, something that will do this to a person – that's the sort of thing we're looking for. But you've done this before. If there's anything there, I need you to find it for me." Tanya left them and headed back to her car.

She was wet to the skin and dirty. She needed to go straight to the office but couldn't remember what clothes she had in her locker. The last time she had been in there had been before her injury. There wasn't time to go home. As the thought crossed her mind, she realised – for the last few hours, she had given no thought at all to her domestic situation. She still had to sort things out about Serena.

She picked up her phone and quickly scanned the messages looking for Fiona's name. There was nothing, not even an acknowledgement of her curt voicemail. With a sigh, she threw the phone onto the passenger seat and drove out of the parking area. Her car jolted and jerked back down the narrow path towards the main road. It would have to be dealt with, but right now the main thing was the case. It was time to mobilise the team, to move forward, and at least find out who had been left in a fishing lake, discarded like a 'bag of rags'.

It was now almost eight-thirty. She called Paul Harris and told him to get the rest of the team organised as quickly as possible. "Kate has things set up in the office.

Operational name is Rambler. There has been a significant development and I'll be there very soon."

* * *

By the time she reached headquarters, they were there. They had already taken up the usual spots, the same desks and when she looked in on her way to her old office, it was to a round of warm greetings. Even Sue Rollinson joined in with an enthusiastic, "Great to see you back, ma'am."

"I'll just drop my bag and get into some dry things, then I'll be back in for a briefing. There's a post-mortem later. Paul, will you attend with me?"

The detective sergeant nodded at her.

The office was in darkness. She turned on the overhead light; her desk waited for her, bare except for a couple of cables ready for her laptop and a landline phone. Standard equipment, even though it was hardly used these days. There were a couple of empty metal trays. It was dusty and neglected looking. Someone had been in while she was away on sick leave and taken away the other workstation – Charlie's desk. The extra space made her feel very alone. She looked at the dings in the carpet and the stain where he had spilled coffee.

Did she need someone; someone to bounce the ideas off? Someone to rant to when things went wrong? There was a time when she would have said, no, she was fine on her own, better in sole charge. But now, because she had come to rely on his quiet resolve, alone didn't seem quite enough.

She could hear them in the squad room. They were a good team but none of them was Charlie. She shook off the gloom, now wasn't the time to turn soft. She stamped along the corridor and pulled jeans and a grey wool sweater from her locker. They were reasonably clean but smelled fusty. It wouldn't have to matter – she sprayed some deodorant around. She was ready.

Time to get to work.

When the office door opened, she expected Kate, or maybe Paul, not the tall dark-haired stranger who nodded at her and stepped into the room. "DI Miller?" he asked.

She nodded, and he walked towards her, his hand extended.

"DS Finch. Brian." He glanced around. "So, in here or out there?" He waved a hand towards the corridor leading to the incident room.

"What, wait. I don't understand."

"Oh." He blushed, stretched his lips in a grimace. "Awkward!" he said. "I thought you'd been informed. I'm supposed to join the team. DCI Scunthorpe said he'd let you know. I'm in limbo a bit. Just taken my Inspector's thing." He held up his hand, fingers crossed. "Should be okay I think, but until I have the result…"

Tanya glanced down at her phone. There hadn't been any messages from the DCI. She hadn't had a chance to check her email properly. Even so, this wasn't right. She should have been properly informed, introduced. Maybe she should even have been involved in the decision. She felt a flash of irritation. She would speak to the DCI, but not now. For now, the main thing was to get the others organised, try and bring in some civilian assistants to go through the CCTV and Traffic Cameras, and then go to the post-mortem.

She frowned at Finch. It wasn't his fault. "Look, there are spare desks in the other room. Can you sort yourself out? This is all still early stages."

She could tell by his face that she had offended him; he had expected a more friendly reception. Not the best start to a working relationship. She closed her eyes briefly. She'd messed up the personnel side of things again, hadn't she? She summoned up a weak smile and held out her hand. "Sorry, sorry. Welcome on board. It's all a bit confused and rushed right now. We'll have to have a chat. Later, yeah?"

He shook her hand, picked up his bag and walked to the door. "I'll just go and find a place to park myself then." He left the room.

Shit, Bob, thanks a lot.

Chapter 12

The newcomer had dumped his bag on a spare desk in the corner and, when Tanya joined them, had already introduced himself, shaking hands with the rest of the team. Sue Rollinson handed him a cup of coffee. Tanya swallowed a grin. The young woman wasn't wasting any time. Mind, he was easy on the eye, this newcomer. Tall, dark-haired, fit looking with a ready smile; and his suit and tie made Paul's jeans and hoody look decidedly shabby. Then again Paul was decidedly shabby.

Dan Price turned as Tanya moved towards the whiteboard and raised his eyebrows at her. She smiled back at him. He was more comfortable with them now. Now they all knew that he was gay and accepted him totally. He had let go of some of his natural diffidence and she was sure, as his confidence grew, he would do well in his career. He was sharp and keen.

"Okay, sorry about this, guys. This is Detective Sergeant Brian Finch, soon to be Inspector Finch."

The new member of the team gave a quiet laugh and raised crossed fingers.

"I didn't have the chance to introduce him properly."

DS Finch knew that it was because she hadn't been forewarned. It would be a test of his discretion if he kept that fact to himself.

"Sorry, boss, I introduced myself. Thought it would save some time."

"That's great, thanks, Detective Sergeant. Things are moving fast. You've arrived along with this new development, so familiarise yourself with the body." Tanya pointed at the hideous pictures that Kate had posted on the whiteboard. "We don't have much more than that. I think it would be best if you come with Detective Sergeant Harris and myself to the post-mortem exam. And then you'll be up to date."

He nodded.

"Right, now," Tanya addressed them all, "as you've heard we've found a head. Don't have many details yet. However, for the moment it makes sense to assume it's from our victim. I need more detailed interviews with the members at the golf club. Ask about strangers hanging around, unusual activity around that tee. Is that what you call it? Whatever. But wait until we see what this new find can tell us. With luck it might bring us nearer to an identification. I'd be grateful for anything at the moment."

She turned to Detective Lewis, "Kate, can you have some of the civilians viewing CCTV of the wider area for the past week? If we can match a car from the golf club with one anywhere near the lake that would be a big move forward, but really anything that seems odd. The club, the lake, and all points in between. After the morgue, I'm going back to do the interviews with our two original witnesses, the blokes who found the body. They may have remembered something else, but as they found this poor sod days after he was dumped there, I'm not hopeful. To be honest guys, just now, we have nothing. So, think outside the box."

She was aware of Finch's eyes on her the whole time. She couldn't shake the feeling that he was judging her and

assessing her performance. She was irritated that he had
arrived the way that he had. She texted a message to DCI
Scunthorpe's office requesting a meeting as soon as
possible.

Chapter 13

Before she had a chance to put it away, the phone vibrated, and Tanya was surprised to see Simon Hewitt's ID. She glanced around the room. "I'll take this. Hold on." She listened without comment, but as she slid it back into her pocket, she sighed and rubbed a hand over her face.

The team watched in silence, and tension rose in the room as she moved towards the whiteboards. "Right, that was the morgue. They've extracted the head from its sack. The other objects in there, were, as expected – hands. Two." She paused a moment. "The head is female." She let the hubbub break around her, using the moment to try and still her own seething thoughts.

Paul Harris was the one who put it into words. "Well, that's put the cat among the pigeons …make no mistake."

"You could say that. Two separate discoveries, two crime scenes. I need to get on to DCI Scunthorpe; we need the divers back in the lake – they need to do the whole area, now they are looking for a body."

She glanced at Kate Lewis who nodded. "Dr Hewitt thinks there could be a chance of identification through the teeth. They're taking impressions and photographs now. Paul, you need to get over there."

She turned to the newcomer. "Will you go as well, get me whatever you can, about both of them. I'll have to stay here and speak to DCI Scunthorpe, we'll need more help, more civilians at least. I want you to see if they can produce an image of this woman's face that is viewable. We can put out an appeal on the media. Apparently, there wasn't a great deal of decomposition as the water is cold at this time of the year. There's not too much we can do immediately, but as soon as we have age and nationality, I want you, Detective Constables Rollinson and Price, hunting through misper reports for the last three weeks. They say that any longer than that there would have been more decay."

Sue Rollinson raised a hand. "What if the head wasn't put into the water straight away, ma'am?"

"Yes, of course, we are only at the starting point. We will go further back as we need to; we have to bear that in mind." Tanya turned to the door. "Dr Hewitt will be able to give you an idea, I should think. If the victim was previously kept somewhere else, then the decay will have been different. Find out."

"What about the hands? In the sack?" Kate Lewis spoke up again. "Were they the hands to match the head or…? Well, what I mean is, the body had no head and no hands. This head has nothing. Oh lord, you know what I mean."

"They're examining the hands separately and Dr Hewitt wouldn't comment. He hasn't had a chance to look at them closely yet. That's something else for you two," she said, addressing the men. "Please don't come back and tell me they don't match! Okay, for now, these are two completely separate cases. We're not going to jump to any conclusions. Start another record, Kate, another board; and I suppose we need another operational name. Right, let's move on this. I'm going to the office now and then I'll join you at the morgue."

She called towards the two figures disappearing into the corridor. "I'll be right behind you. The witness interviews can be put on the back burner, at least until we have more information."

The unforeseen arrival of Detective Sergeant Finch suddenly seemed fortuitous; with two bodies and two cases, she would need all the help that she could get. She really didn't want to let either of the cases go to another team. She had been in at the start. As far as Tanya was concerned, that meant they were hers.

Chapter 14

By the time she had walked to DCI Scunthorpe's office, Tanya was pretty much over the earlier anger. She needed the extra help now and at the end of the day, it was the DCI's decision as to the relocation of officers. Okay, he hadn't informed her, but what the hell did it matter? There were more important things to worry about.

He offered her coffee, but she refused, she didn't have the time. When he began to tell her about the new team member, she cut him off. "He's already with us, sir."

"Ah, sorry about that. He was due later today. Ha, good to see that he's keen."

"I'm glad of the help, sir. There's been a major development and we're going to be pushed to manage with the numbers we have now, including Detective Sergeant Finch."

She told him about the gender of the head and possibly the hands. "There's no way to know yet whether there is a link between the two discoveries, but the locations are close, so it's more than possible, I think. But, for now, we really have to treat them as two separate incidents, until something tells us different."

DCI Scunthorpe nodded. He glanced down at the file open on his desk. "He comes with great references, Finch. Good computer skills. I know you've got Detective Constable Lewis, but he's got the advanced quals and what have you – a degree, you know. We are just waiting for his promotion to come through; needed somewhere to park him."

"Yes, sir, he did say." She struggled to hide her irritation. "Detective Lewis is really competent, sir. I know she hasn't got formal qualifications or anything, but she has experience and a natural talent. I value her highly."

Scunthorpe waved a hand. "Yes, I know. I'm aware of Kate's strengths, but another head can't hurt in this situation." He looked Tanya in the eye, daring her to grin. "Sorry, poor choice of words. Can you handle them both, the body and now this other thing? I could arrange for another team to handle the second discovery?"

"I'd rather manage them both, sir. If they are connected, then it'll be quicker because we'll be up to speed on all the facts."

"Good point. I'll see what I can do about bringing in some more people to help with screening for cars and so on." He paused. "Is everything okay at home for you now, Tanya? With your niece?"

Again, mention of her personal situation was like a slap in the face; she had forgotten about Serena. "Yes, it's fine, sir. She's going back to Scotland." As she said it, she knew it had to be true, there was no room for any more complications. She would call Fiona again as soon as she had a moment. She would just tell her she was putting the girl on a train tomorrow, end of.

* * *

Back at the incident room, the team were quiet and focused. Kate and Sue barely glanced up as she walked in. She looked at her watch. There was still time to drive over to the morgue, the post-mortem on the body would most likely be in full swing and she could get a proper look at the head. Then again, if she did, maybe it would look as though she was checking up on the new guy – not a good idea. She sent a text to Paul Harris explaining that she had changed her plans and would meet them back at headquarters. She reminded them to send through images as soon as possible.

She would wait, go back to her own office and update her paperwork. She would telephone home and tell Serena to sort and pack her things, ring Scotland and get that out of the way.

Her office door was already open and a couple of men in overalls were busy locating a new desk. Computer equipment and a chair stood in the middle of the room. "What's this?"

"Desk for DI Finch. Can you sign for it, ma-am?" He held out an electronic tablet and Tanya scrawled across it with the plastic stick.

"Who requisitioned it?" she asked.

"Dunno, we just deliver 'em, set 'em up."

"And it's Detective Inspector Finch?"

"That's what it says on the docket." The technician waved a piece of paper.

So, his results had come through.

Well, he'd needed a desk and now he had one; maybe Kate had ordered it. Presumptuous and unlike her, but then perhaps she'd been instructed. Had he told the team about his promotion and cut her out? Yes, she was annoyed, but what really was the problem? It was a desk, just a bloody desk. Tanya went out into the corridor to phone home in the relative quiet.

The land line rang out until the messaging machine cut in; and Serena's mobile was unanswered. Tanya left a message for the girl to call her as soon as possible. She toyed with the idea of telling her to sort out her things ready to go, but it seemed heartless, and Serena hadn't been that bad. Not until the last week or so anyway.

Chapter 15

As the morning wore on, Ana had begun to feel unwell. Whatever had caused Emilia to cough and shiver must have attacked her now. She was aching and hot. She looked at the clock at the end of the big room. Just four hours and then it would be time to go home. She could do four hours; she had put up with much worse.

She glanced around the noisy, stinking place. They would probably all get the sickness now. It would go on and on and nobody would be able to take time off, not until they were unable to clamber into the van at any rate.

Pietre, the young lad who had joined them last month, smiled at her. She managed to summon up a smile for him; he was still hopeful and still believed that this was a means to an end. He reminded her of her brother. At the thought of her brother and her mother back in their scruffy little house, her throat filled with a lump of pain. She had done all of this for them. That had been the plan at any rate. Now look. All it had done really was to put them in danger.

Dani didn't have family now. Her mother had died and that had been the key to her decision to escape. Elian? None of them knew about him. They knew that he had arrived with drugs still in his belly, and when they had been shat out, he had joined the men in the old house. He had been so trusting, loving really, and he had been treated kindly by his housemates. But when she had decided to go, Dani just took him because she could. He didn't know enough to refuse, and he would be like some sort of security for her, big as he was, broad on the shoulders, and tall.

Well, if he had family at home, they would suffer now, but it couldn't be helped. None of it. When they first disappeared, there had been hell to pay; shouting and kicking, but, in the end, nobody had really known anything. The thugs had given up and it all calmed down again. Dani hadn't told anyone except Ana what she had been planning, and even that was just that she was going – no hint of where, no hint of when.

The bell rang for a toilet break and she swallowed two paracetamols with cold water straight from the tap. She could manage the rest of the day and then she would sleep. She remembered how her mother would make soup if she was ill – soup and hot drinks – and wrap a scarf around her neck. She remembered how she would sing to her when she was small, stroking her forehead and murmuring until she drifted off to sleep. Nothing could happen to Mama, nothing; so, she would endure and maybe, one day it would all be over – one way or another. Maybe one day she would really have paid for her transport and her papers; maybe one day it would all come true and she could go to London, find Dani and they could look for work together, and their lives would be worth living again. Maybe.

Chapter 16

By the time Paul Harris and Brian Finch arrived back at the office, the images from the post-mortem on the cadaver, and the examination of the head and hands, were being posted onto the whiteboard.

Tanya watched the two detectives, they looked pale. Before he spoke to anyone, Paul Harris filled the kettle, kept against regulations on a table in the corner. "Tea or coffee, boss?"

Tanya was about to tell him that she didn't want a hot drink then realised he was addressing Brian Finch. So, they all knew.

"Coffee please; black, two sugars. Thanks. I need a real drink after that, but I guess coffee will do for now." He crossed the room to where Tanya had turned back to the board.

"Bit grim, was it?" she asked him.

"Well to be fair it's never pleasant, I don't think."

She couldn't tell him that mostly she just felt interest and excitement. That nothing of the dead person seemed to be in the room with them, only the inhuman remains. It was something she had tried to explain now and then, and nobody understood. Other people thought her cold and unnatural, perhaps a bit ghoulish. But it wasn't that. She saw it all – the crime scene, the post-mortem, the disturbing images – as a means to an end; part of the puzzle that would help her win justice for the victims. In the field it was different, there was still something of the human being there, maybe the twist of limbs, some personal effects. But once they were inside the morgue, they became another thing altogether. One day she might speak to Simon Hewitt about it, ask him if it was really so unnatural not to be upset by it. For now, though, she just gave a nod and made a noise that she hoped would sound like agreement.

"Somehow it was worse," Finch said, "no head, you know. I kept finding myself looking at the empty space. Really strange. Anyway…" He accepted the coffee from Paul Harris.

The others had gathered around by now and he addressed the group. "Dr Hewitt is sending his reports as soon as possible. A Dr Lee did the examination on the hands and he's including her findings, thought it would make it easier for us if it all came together. The male…" He opened his notebook. "Young, probably mid-twenties. Pubic and body hair was dark, therefore it's reasonable to assume the hair on the head was dark, always excluding chemical alteration of course. Fairly big, but in an overweight way, rather than muscular. In spite of his size, poor bone density and other things indicated malnutrition, 'a bit fat but not well fed,' was how it was explained. From the measurements of the long bones he was just around one point eight metres – that's around six feet in old money." He glanced at Kate as he said it.

Tanya cringed inwardly. Detective Constable Lewis was reasonably easy going, but she was sensitive about being the oldest member of the team.

Brian Finch continued, unaware of causing any offence. "Signs of a couple of badly healed fractures – ribs – probably from childhood. One of the most interesting things was the removal of the hands. Dr Hewitt said the cuts were fairly clean. Not sawn and thankfully post-mortem. He reckons a weighty, sharp object, something like an axe, and delivered with a heavy blow. Apart from that, he wasn't telling us much more. This led to the medical examiner concluding that death was most likely caused by injury to the head. More than that he couldn't say until we find said missing part and he can have a look. Samples have been sent for toxicology and DNA. No signs of long-term drug or alcohol use. No tattoos or whatever. So, that's about it for him."

He continued, "The head. A female, as we know. She had longish, dark hair. The eyes were gone. Probably eaten by creatures in the water. The teeth are our best bet for identification there, though the gums had degraded. They've taken dental impressions and pictures. Dr Hewitt reckons that from the look of the work done, which was just a few fillings, she was probably not from the UK originally. The standard of dentistry wasn't what he would expect, but he's taken samples of the amalgam for further investigation."

He now addressed Tanya directly. "I've arranged to have the details circulated among our colleagues in Europe, and when the image of her face is ready, that is going to be sent on as well. She didn't look that good in the flesh, as it were, but they're convinced they'll be able to produce something that looks like her and isn't too grim for the public to see. That should be coming over in a couple of hours. So, that's the outline of what we know. Oh sorry, the hands. Again, a heavy, sharp object such as an axe. They were almost certainly a match for the head – that's to be finally confirmed by the lab, but it doesn't make any sense at all if not – female, probably the same age, the right size."

"Thank God for that," Tanya said.

"Quite. The nails were short and broken, not 'professionally' manicured at all." He made air quotes with his fingers. "They had been painted red. They have taken samples of the polish in the hope that we might be able to trace it. It's a long shot though, there's thousands of different bottles of the stuff. Callouses on the palms and healing cuts on several fingers. The thinking is that she had been doing some sort of manual work prior to death."

"Okay." Tanya glanced around the team. "I'm not sure that gets us much further. We've got the same or similar weapon, so that's a link."

"If the head is from someone not from here, I mean, not English," Sue Rollinson said, "and the body is malnourished, that's another sort of link, isn't it?"

"How so?" Tanya asked her.

"Well, I know that these days there are major problems with kids not being fed properly. Schools are talking about it all the time, aren't they? But it's relatively recent in this country. Since the financial crash, austerity, this bloody government." There were a couple of grunts of agreement. She continued. "Mid-twenties, that puts him as a child just after the turn of the century. I don't think it was that bad then, was it? I was a kid, we had plenty to eat, vitamins from the clinic – I remember my mum getting those."

"Okay, where is this taking you?" Tanya said.

"Well, the woman's teeth say she's possibly not English. Do the poor bone strength and signs of malnutrition say the same thing? It's weak I know but maybe it's worth considering."

Tanya nodded. "It does start to look as though these two are connected in death, because of the weapon and the removal of body parts. It will be a big help if we can connect them in life as well."

"That's good thinking, Rollinson," Brian Finch said.

Sue's dark complexion darkened even more as she smiled back at the DI. Tanya stifled a groan. So much for Constable Rollinson's lifelong affection for Charlie Lambert – he hadn't been gone more than a couple of months and here she was simpering in front of his replacement.

"Right. Sue, you come with me. We'll go back out and interview the secretary of the golf club. See if he's been employing any foreign workers. The rest of you get back to the search for cars moving between the two areas, probably at night of course. Tossing a bag of body parts into a lake during the day seems a bit far-fetched. Kate can you chase up the reports and make sure everyone who should have one is in the loop. We haven't got much, but we've just got to keep on digging. Detective Inspector Finch, could I have a word in my office before I leave? Oh yeah, our office, your new desk has arrived. Thanks for that, Kate."

"Sorry, ma'am?" The woman shook her head in confusion.

"I sorted it," Brian Finch said, "I just made a couple of calls. I hope that's okay."

"Oh, yes. Of course. Well, I suppose this would be a good time for you to get settled in. I'm going home after the interviews at the golf club. Some stuff to sort out. Sue, follow me in your old banger. Afterwards, I'll be available on the usual systems, so if anything pops up let me know immediately. If not, back in tomorrow, half seven, for a catch up."

"If anyone fancies a drink after shift, I wouldn't mind getting acquainted with the local watering holes. My shout, bit of a celebration." Finch said. He lowered his head and gave them a grin.

"Yeah, I'm up for that, and congratulations, sir," Paul Harris answered.

Finch waved a hand dismissively.

"Count me in." No surprise there from Sue.

Kate just shook her head. "Sorry, can't tonight, but yeah, congratulations, sir."

Dan waited a moment and glanced at his watch. "Yes, okay, just a quick one," he said.

Brian Finch followed Tanya along the short corridor; he closed the door and waited for her to speak.

"We haven't had much chance to get you familiarised with the team and so on. Perhaps tomorrow, early, before the meeting I could give you a rundown. Seems as though you've already got arrangements for this evening."

Tanya was just having a dig because she was well aware that the evening for her, was going to be full of Serena, and Fiona, and family stuff that she could very well do without just now. But she wondered about Brian Finch's timing. He had mentioned going for a drink after she had already told them she was going home. Did he want to have the team to himself? Or was she reading something into an innocent coincidence? She held out her hand. "Oh yes, of course, congratulations on the promotion," she said.

"Thanks. DCI Scunthorpe had a word earlier, we agreed that I'll stay on with you for now. He said you'd told him you've been needing help."

That wasn't what she had said, wasn't at all what she had meant, but there was no way out of this now. "Right, fine."

"It'll be good to have a chat with the troops tonight, casually you know, and I did a bit of research on them when I knew I was joining you."

"How long ago was that?" Tanya asked.

"Couple of days – pretty much when you picked up the case really. I'd just come back on board. I've been away on a couple of courses, Nottingham Uni, then the inspector's exam and… Look, it's fine. I'll just have a natter with them all tonight. We've got plenty of other stuff to get on with, after all."

She couldn't argue but his attitude irritated her. She knew that she had never been a good team player, but it was usual to have a debrief with a new senior. His mistake with Kate was an example of what could happen with a newcomer to an established team. It was annoying and unsettling, but the force was struggling, it was no secret, and this was no time to stand on ceremony. She had to just move on. She felt oddly insecure in the face of his confidence. He was already at an advantage purely as an accident of gender.

She picked up her coat and bag and turned to look at his workstation, now all set up. The desk looked new, the computer equipment was better than hers, the screen larger, slicker. She pushed these petty thoughts aside. They had to work together, but she wished it was Charlie in the office with her right now.

As she walked into the corridor, she narrowly avoided collision with a maintenance man who was slotting a new name plate into the holder on the wall outside her office. 'Detective Inspector Brian Finch'.

She stomped down the corridor muttering under her breath. Sue Rollinson was standing beside her old second-hand car, a cast-off given to her by one of her brothers. The other woman grinned and waved, Tanya raised a hand as she slid into her own vehicle and slammed her door. Sue might be taken in by his good looks and friendly manner, but she had a horrible feeling that the new officer had brought conflict with him.

Chapter 17

Steven Traynor was no help at all, he was nervous and edgy even as he showed them into the office in the clubhouse. His hands on the desk in front of him twitched; the fingers knitting and twisting constantly. Tanya's eyes were drawn to them, squirming on the cheap wooden surface like two little creatures fighting to escape. His nails were bitten and on one thumb was a small, sore looking place where it appeared that he had chewed at the cuticle and made it bleed.

She made no attempt to put him at his ease; if this man had something to hide, she needed to get at it.

He had never employed foreign staff, he told them. Cleaners were from the local area. He waved a hand in the direction of the block of flats on the other side of the narrow road outside. They came and went, and he promised to provide a list covering the past two years. The groundskeepers – a chief keeper and two juniors – were all long-serving members, and Traynor assured the police officers that he knew them well; they were from Oxford town. He had given their details to the sergeant already and would vouch for them all with no hesitation.

"They're qualified, experienced. We don't employ casuals, people don't understand the skill required," he said. For a moment anger had flared.

The only other regular staff member was the bar manager whom they had already met.

"Jamie, you've met him," Traynor said, "lovely bloke. Been with us for a couple of years now. Originally from up north somewhere, Liverpool maybe. Yes, Liverpool somewhere."

"So, there have never been any casual staff who might have been from outside the UK?" Tanya asked.

He shook his head. "No, none. We've never needed anyone else. We run a tight ship here. Regulated."

He was all nerves and edginess, but as far as the current questions were concerned, she didn't think he was lying. It was easy to check after all.

As they walked back to the car park, she questioned Sue. "What did you think?"

"I think he's hiding something, but I couldn't get a bead on it, ma'am. He was very nervous."

"Yes, I think it might be worth our while to bring him in to the station. Tomorrow, in the afternoon. Can you arrange that? Helping with our enquiries, that sort of thing. I think if we rattle him, something might shake loose. Just a feeling but worth following up, I reckon."

"Ma'am."

"Right, I'm going home. It's nearly knocking off time anyway. Are you going back to the office? You can go home if you like, as long as you're contactable," Tanya said.

"I'm going back, boss. Out for a drink with the new DI, remember?"

"Oh yes, I'd forgotten."

"Why don't you come? It'll be good to have a get together. The last one was when Charlie left."

"No, I've got stuff to deal with at home," Tanya said.

The other woman shrugged and let it go.

Tanya tried to concentrate on what waited for her at home. She would call and get some pizza. Tonight's conversation might be tricky, but Serena had been through the mill and was deserving of kindness, especially from her own family. There was no getting away from it, she was family. Small and dysfunctional it might be but, despite her efforts to break free, the ties still held her. Surely there was no need for it to be dreadful and antagonistic. They needed to get back to the way it had been, with the occasional visit or phone call.

She walked into the house via the door to the kitchen. It was clean and tidy; she allowed a smile. This might not be too bad, and it was well past time to finish this episode. "Serena, I'm back. I hope you're hungry," she called out.

There was no answer.

Chapter 18

There was no music, no smell of toast or coffee, which seemed to be a staple of her niece's life. Lights were burning, but only the ones set on timers. As Tanya walked across the hall and into the living room, she knew already that the house was empty.

Anger flared. She had been clear. She had told the girl to stay at home. It wasn't late. There was food and comfort, no reason for her to have gone anywhere. Tanya sighed. She went back into the kitchen and turned the oven on low. She slid the pizza in to keep warm.

Though she knew already that it was a waste of time she shouted up the stairs, "Serena. I'm back." Of course, there was no response and she didn't even bother to go to the bedroom. Not until she noticed that both of the girl's jackets were missing from the hall stand. There were no trainers or shoes under the shelf. The hairs on the back of her neck prickled. "Oh, shit."

Now she ran up the stairs and burst into the guest room. The wardrobes were empty, the bed was rumpled and unmade. Tanya closed her eyes for a moment and tried to calm her breathing. So, the stupid girl had either pulled another disappearing act –surely not, not after last time – or... Her mind was blank, and then she saw the note on the dresser.

> *Tanya*
> *I have taken my daughter home. It is obvious that you have had enough of helping your family. You never were particularly reliable. I have cancelled the standing order for her keep.*
> *Fiona*

That was it, no 'thank you', nothing at all from Serena herself. Although it had been exactly what Tanya was hoping for, it was gutting. They had never been close, and even though she had saved the family from tragedy, Tanya had left Scotland on bad terms with her sister. A few steps in the right direction had been made in the past few weeks, but now, well now, it seemed it was all over.

She didn't know how to feel. Their parents had been dead for a while. With no other siblings, Fiona was the only link with a past that Tanya remembered as a long succession of disappointment and anger. She had been the second best, the 'also ran'. Now, here was an opportunity that she had believed she had always wanted. Total freedom from her younger self. This could be the end of any residual sense of duty. But, inexplicably, she felt hurt and sad.

Then, of course, there was the final line in the note. The cancellation of the standing order. Fiona had been generous. Maybe guilt, possibly genuine gratitude. Whatever the reason, the money had been a lifeline for Tanya. Her overdraft, which was recently arranged, was already stretched to the limit. She had reasoned that it was there to use so she might as well use it, but incredibly quickly the extra couple of thousand had been swallowed up. Boredom during her sick leave had placed her in front of the computer, and again the online shops had been too much temptation. She had been relying on the money from her sister, far more than she would spend on food for Serena, and now it was gone.

She didn't need to log on and look at her bank statement to know that the next mortgage and utilities payment would plunge her back into the red. On one level she knew her thinking was selfish and she ought to be more upset about the rift in her family, but that wasn't the way it was.

She turned around and left the room, the bed unmade, the curtains open, and stomped back down the stairs.

In the living room, with the pizza on the table in front of her, she logged on to her laptop and opened her notes. Her sister and niece could look after themselves, she would handle the financial problems in due course; for now, she had to do her job. It was the one area where she could not allow herself to fail.

Chapter 19

Ana pulled the duvet close around her chin. The day had seemed endless. By the time the van dropped herself and Emilia back at the caravan she was shivering, coughing, and every joint ached. She had taken some more paracetamol and pleaded with the driver to arrange for a doctor for herself and Emi, or at least to bring them some stronger medicine; she asked for antibiotics.

He had sneered at her. "Better you drink hot tea, get in your bed. Be ready for work tomorrow. There are no medicines, this is England – there is no doctor unless you are official. You are trouble now and we don't need trouble. You stop being trouble, yes?"

With that, he had clambered back into the old VW and slammed the door. The comment about doctors worried her, she had been told that in England everyone could have health care, even the very poor. It was another lie.

Bogdan had never been kind, not from the first day when he had picked her up from the ferry and thrown her bags into the boot of a clapped-out old car. But now, both he and his mate – another bulky, rough thug – were worse every day. She would have appealed to his kinder side but was convinced that, if he had ever had one, it had been brutalised out of him. Maybe the war, maybe fear and worry, or perhaps he had always been a heartless bully. She could try and charm him, offer to give him the only thing she had, but the idea of sex disgusted her, and it would start down a road that she knew would only lead to more torment, more degradation.

The bullying was worse since Dani and Elian had gone. Maybe the men had been held responsible and punished. Probably there would be more repercussions, probably things would never improve, and she was here now in this stinking little place becoming more and more unhealthy, more and more desperate, and perhaps soon she would die. Thoughts of death were often with her and she could never be sure whether it was fear or longing that was the overriding feeling.

She wondered what they would do then. Would they send her body home? She couldn't imagine them spending the money. Would they leave her at a hospital, a police station, maybe a church? At least at a church they would take care of her body and maybe her blackened soul. In her fevered mind, the thoughts grew until she was convinced that she would succumb to whatever was ailing her. The idea of her body being discarded somewhere in this inhospitable, foreign country segued into nightmares and she tossed and twisted under the thin duvet. In her tortured sleep the tears leaked from under her eyelids to soak the pillow.

In the early hours, she opened her eyes. The night was silent, she was no longer shivering, and her fever had broken. She slid from the bed, filled a cup with cold water from the tap, and swallowed more pills. There was no sound from the other end of the place, not even the snoring she was used to, and there was a moment of panic. But then the rustle of bedding reassured her that Emilia was still alive.

With the thought, her dream came back. The image of her body, naked and undignified in the gutter. A crowd gathered around, peering down at her, pointing and shaking their heads in disgust. She had seen such things herself, but that had been in a country at war, not here; not in this green and pleasant land.

She bent and dragged her bag from under the bed. Her few clean clothes were stored in there already, and it took just a couple of minutes, working by the light of the moon through the window, to push in the other few bits she cared about.

The door was locked. She knew that every night the thugs did rounds when it was growing dark. They secured the caravans and she had heard them shouting at the men in the cottage. But this was a thin, feeble door. They didn't imagine any of the women would risk running. They had faith in the power of their threats. Dani and Elian had slipped away from the factory during the day. They had left with nothing, but they had disappeared during one of the toilet breaks. It wasn't until the evening that it was noticed they were missing. Dani had tried to tell her the plan, explained that she had hidden things in readiness, but Ana had refused to listen. She had been too afraid to know anything. In truth, she had never really believed the other woman would go. But she had, and they hadn't brought them back. So, it seemed that, in spite of everything, it was possible to escape. Dani and Elian had proved it and if they could do it, so could she.

The door lock proved tougher than it appeared, and she had to give up. But the window frames were old and warped. She climbed onto the bed and levered the handle of a spoon under the aluminium.

"Ana?" The quiet murmur from the other side of the room stopped her for a moment.

She spoke in their native language thinking it would be more comforting. "It's okay, Emi, I just need some air. Go back to sleep. It's okay. Sorry I woke you." She waited, quietly, not moving, hardly daring to breathe, until at last, she heard guttural snoring.

The sky was lightening outside, and she had to hurry now. The thin handle of the spoon bent in her hand and she pushed it back into shape. She could feel a draught under the corner of the window as she worked at it with the thin metal, prising and twisting. It wasn't making enough difference. Of course, she realised, this wasn't the way. She must work on the lock, on the middle of the frame.

She moved along the bed, feeling with her fingertips until she found the edge of what was left of the lock. The little handle had been sawn away on the inside. It had never been intended for the residents to open it. If it had been screwed closed, or glued maybe, then she was lost. The draught she had felt on her fingers from the corner gave her small hope. She pushed the handle of the spoon under the lock. It bent again, and when she tried to straighten it, the thin metal snapped. She peered down at the two pieces in her hand and let out a sob of frustration. She could break the window; she could hammer at it with her shoe. But then Emi would wake, and anyway, the driver's own caravan —a smarter, warmer, better one, almost a little bungalow – was too near. He would hear, his big dog would hear. He prowled at night with the animal; she had seen him through the thin curtain, pacing across the grass, the red glow of his cigarette flaring as he inhaled. The thought of him and the big black animal made her sob. If he found her outside, she knew he would be enraged.

She shook her head, there was nothing left to lose. Once she was free, she would have to call Mama, to tell her brother that they were in danger, give them a chance to take precautions. Then it could all be alright. Not the bright future that they had wished for, but better than this. Even going back to the poverty at home would be better than this. First though, to get free.

She tried again to lever the window frame. As it flexed and bent, tiny pieces of dried out sealant fell on the back of her hand. She brushed them aside impatiently until more crumbled and she understood it was the answer.

Chipping and picking with the broken end of the spoon handle made short work of the old, rotten filler. Then she felt the Perspex of the window shift and move as the crumbled dust fell down onto her bed.

With a swift glance at the dark hump of the sleeping Emilia, she leaned against the pane and pushed from the corners. She wasn't afraid it would shatter as glass would have done, but she didn't want to risk it jamming half in and half out, foiling her escape and worse, showing how she had tried. She thumped at it sharply with the heels of her hands.

In the event, it popped out in one piece and landed with a dull thud onto the grass at the back of the caravan. She pushed her bag through and slid out of her jacket, also bundling it outside.

She had lost weight since her arrival and now she was glad of her new skinny, bony frame. The womanly body that she had when she left home would never have been able to squirm and wriggle through this space. She went through head first, but knew at once that it had been a mistake. It was too late. All she could do was push and heave her way forward until her hips were through and she was braced against the side of the van with her straining arms on the outside and her bent knees holding her against the interior. It wasn't far to the ground and with one final heave, and a thrust with her legs, she let herself fall, tucking in her head as she tumbled onto the damp grass.

She rolled to her feet, grabbed her things, and without a glance back, she ran across the narrow area between the caravan and the hedge. She forced through, scratching her hands and head on the thorns, protecting her face with her jacket, but then her feet hit the tarmac of the road. For a moment she hesitated, dragging on the nylon coat, and then, for no other reason than it was the direction of the sunrise, she turned to the right and ran, her breath clouding the air in front of her, her shoes thudding on the hard ground. She was free.

Chapter 20

Tanya's house felt unnaturally quiet in the early morning. She had been irritated often by the sound of music from Serena's room, she had been annoyed by the messy evidence of overnight snacks in the kitchen, but now that it was her own again, the place felt somehow depleted.

Not bothering with breakfast, she bought a takeaway latte and a muffin on the way into the office. From the first day of working together, she and Charlie Lambert had shared this routine. Today she didn't buy a second pastry for Brian Finch… she considered it, but only briefly.

When she walked into the office, she was glad she hadn't bothered. In the corner, on a small table, was a shiny coffee maker, a box of coffee pods and a carton of milk. The air smelled of coffee and croissants.

As she plugged in her laptop and logged on to check the overnight reports, she heard footsteps in the corridor. She popped off the lid from her cup and held it in her hand, sipping as he walked through the door, and she scrolled through the list of occurrences.

"Morning, Tanya," Finch said.

She glanced up and nodded. Again, he was dressed in a suit and he slipped the jacket off to hang it on the coat stand. She frowned, *since when did they have a coat stand?* His shirt and tie were immaculate, his hair styled and gelled. So, yesterday's neat turnout hadn't been him trying to make an impression. She wondered if a bit of this might rub off on Paul Harris. Probably not, she had never seen the detective sergeant in anything but jeans and a hoody; just cleaner, smarter ones on the couple of occasions when they had met socially. She doubted that he even owned a suit. Perhaps his wedding one from a year or so past, but even then, she wouldn't put money on it. Perhaps he'd worn his uniform – she grinned at the thought.

She nodded. "Detective Inspector. Did you have a good evening, out with the troops?"

"Yes, it was fun. They seem like a tight team, in spite of the recent hiatus. That's down to you, I reckon. We ended up talking about the case, I always think that's a good sign. They're focused."

She ignored the compliment. She had never known how to react to praise – there had been so very little in her past. Not until she had passed out from the police college had her mother at last been proud of her.

"We need to move this on though, don't we?" she said. "We have next to nothing up to now. There's no ID for either victim, no weapon, no real idea of motive. I'm open to any and all ideas. Did anyone have any flashes of inspiration?"

He pursed his lips and shook his head. "Not really, it was just round and round to be honest. Quite a lot of 'what ifs', but nothing we could really work with."

"Okay, so today I'm going back to the golf club. I'd like you to come with me and see where the first body was found – it would be good for you to visit the location. We'll go on to the lake after that. The dive team are probably going to finish there today and up to now they've found nothing." As she spoke, she began to collect her things together.

"Later, I'm going to re-interview the two blokes who found the body. They might have seen something in the time before the storm, and I'm sure they've been mulling it over. They were both pretty shocked, they won't have been able to forget it, and something might have clicked with them," Tanya continued.

It was well known that witnesses often remembered details days after they had been interviewed and were unwilling or embarrassed to get in touch.

"We'll have the rest of the team telephone the other golf club and fishing club members with the same enquiry. I don't want the civilians doing it, they can keep on with the CCTV viewing. I think people take it more seriously if they have a copper on the phone. We're looking for anything at all in the last month. People loitering, anyone who doesn't fit; anything at all. You know, dumps of litter, piles of fag ends, stuff like that. We did a fingertip search after the discovery in the hut, but I'm looking for things from before then. Things that may have been cleared away by the groundsmen, caretakers, even the fishermen at the lake. We need ANPR records from the nearest cameras, so we can try and find the people who've parked or driven past more often than seems normal. There's a restricted exit road from the motorway; we need to find who has access and whether they've noticed anything untoward," she said.

"There are services not all that far away, but we'll get to that. Already it's wide ranging and tedious, needle in a haystack stuff, but we don't have a choice. I'm going to update the DCI now, though I've nothing much to tell him. Can you brief the others, see they're all getting on with it? I'll meet you in the car park, in…" She glanced at her watch. "Fifteen minutes?"

As she finished speaking, she pushed back from her desk, threw the empty coffee cup in the bin and nodded at the table in the corner. "Nice machine."

"Hmm." He glanced across. "Can't stand instant, never could. Help yourself, anytime. There's decaf if you prefer it."

As she left the room, she noticed the discarded box in the corridor. So, he didn't like instant and had splashed out on a new machine for the office. Not a pack of ground coffee, a whole bloody pod machine. "More money than sense." She winced when she heard herself mumbling one of her mother's favourite put-downs.

Chapter 21

Ana ran as far and as fast as was possible. It wasn't very far – she still felt ill and weak. The road was damp with dew and she slowed to a frantic, scuttling walk. She was aware of birdsong; she hadn't heard it for so long. There had been the shriek of gulls at the ferry terminal and now and then chattering in the bushes near the caravan. But the last time she had heard the birds singing had been on the day before she left home, as she had sat with her brother on the steps of their house. They had listened to the local birds going to roost and hadn't realised that it was another pleasure that she was going to relinquish, now all the promises were broken, and all her hopes were betrayed.

The thought of home made her panic. She had to tell them. She had to call her brother in the next hour to let him know they were in danger and he must take Mama and get away. She didn't know where he would go and wouldn't be able to tell him for how long. They couldn't stay at the house. He couldn't work outside – no chopping wood, no foraging. He mustn't be alone in the open. She thought things had reached rock bottom before, but now saw she may take her family even lower before this was all over.

She had her *Halo* card in her bag. She had hidden it there inside a slit in the lining, not because she anticipated what was going to happen to her – she could never have had any idea – but because she soon saw that it was a precious link with home, if ever she had the chance to use it. She had seen a public telephone box in Dover. She recognised it from pictures she had pored over while she waited for the call to travel. She supposed that her phone card would work.

The thugs had taken her own mobile phone away from her, it was one of the first things they did. For safekeeping, they told her and later promised that it would be returned once her debts were paid. That had never happened.

She had to find some houses, some shops, somewhere with a public telephone. She moved on, walking and running in turn until there was the sound of an engine behind her. She turned to peer down the long road and could see a small van in the distance – it was white. She was frozen with fear. Instinct propelled her over a low wall beyond the narrow grass verge. She crouched in the mud and undergrowth until the vehicle, an innocent tradesman's transport that could have taken her away, sped past and left her breathless and panicked at the situation she was in.

Briefly, she considered running back to the caravan, climbing in through the window and wedging the Perspex back in the frame. She could keep the escape route secret until she had a chance to plan, a chance to maybe warn them at home that there was trouble heading their way. Then she thought about the factory, and Emilia's coughing, and the constant sadness and misery, and she clambered back onto the road heading in the direction the van had taken.

The sun was almost up now. There was probably about an hour before the alarm was raised and she didn't know how soon after that they would arrange for someone to take revenge for what she had done.

Maybe Dani was right, and it wasn't true. Maybe they didn't have the means to harm her family. Perhaps that had just been a way of keeping them all in line and there was no danger. Hope flared briefly, and she tamped it down. She couldn't take the risk. She must warn them and then consider her next move. Her next step was to find a way home, or maybe to London where she would find Elian and Dani. She swallowed two of her precious stock of painkillers, pulled her jacket tighter around her shivering body and rushed onwards.

Chapter 22

Peter Baker's face was grey and drawn, his healthy tan had faded, and dark rings sagged under his eyes.

Tanya and DI Brian Finch parked in the road and walked down the wide gravel drive to Baker's impressive, detached house.

The doorbell was answered by a young woman wearing an overall on top of jeans and sweater. They followed her across a square hallway and waited to be admitted to a bright sunroom. Tall windows overlooked the good-sized garden and everywhere spoke of money and luxury. There was a small swimming pool at the other side of a flagged patio and garden furniture grouped around the outside spaces.

Peter Baker sat on a long sofa with his back to the window. On the table in front of him was a glass of water and the remains of a cup of coffee. He stood as they came in and walked towards them like a man much older than his given age of fifty-one.

"Are you okay, Mr Baker?" Tanya asked.

"Not really, no. I'm signed off work, I'm on pills, I feel bloody awful if you must know. I can't close my eyes, every time I do, I see that... the inside of that hut. I can't shut it out. I'm going to see it for the rest of my life. God, how do you people deal with this? How do you un-see that stuff?"

Tanya didn't answer. There wasn't any way to make him feel better.

"We won't keep you long, sir." Finch had led the man back to his seat and now sat opposite to him on a matching sofa.

The detective spoke calmly and quietly. "We find quite often that, as the days go on, witnesses remember things that the shock at the time of an incident has blanked out. We wondered if you had thought of anything more, or whether there had been anything in the days before which had struck you as out of the ordinary?" He opened his notebook. "You had been on the golf course three times in the evenings of the week before the body was found. Did yourself or your golf partner notice anything unusual? Perhaps someone in the vicinity of the hut who shouldn't have been there, anything like that?"

Baker shook his head and cast his eyes downward. "Not that I can remember, no. I'd met with Spencer, it's getting late in the year, but we like to get a game in while we still can. Mostly we played a short round and then had a drink in the clubhouse, and that was that. I didn't notice anything particularly. Now and then there'll be a stranger playing a round but generally it's a well-run club, nobody there that shouldn't be. I can't think of anyone I didn't know, nothing that seemed odd. I'll give it some thought though. I need something to fill my mind." He cleared his throat and Tanya saw the glint of tears in his eyes.

She shifted on the seat and cast a glance towards DI Finch. "Thank you, sir. Look we'll leave you for now. You have my card. If you think of anything at all just give us a call. Are you okay now, is your wife here? Can we get someone for you?"

"No, it's fine. There's just the girl. Tricia is at work. She's been here as much as she can, but she had to go in for a couple of hours. I'm signed off and it leaves the office short-handed, so she's gone in."

"And what is it you do?" Brian Finch had his pen poised above his notebook as he spoke.

"I'm Transport Director, Tricia is Finance. It's her family's company. Woodbarn. Been in the family for generations. It was just a little farm back then. Much bigger now. I need to get back but..." He paused. "Right now, I can't imagine going back to work – back to something ordinary. People will want to talk about it as well. I just can't do that right now. I haven't seen anything in the papers. Tricia told me not to look but I know I won't be able to help myself. Do you know who that poor soul was?"

"Not yet, sir," Tanya said, "it's early days but we're working very hard to find out who he is and what happened.

They left him with his head buried in his hands, struggling to hold himself together. As the cleaner closed the door behind them Brian Finch spoke. "He's pretty shaken up, isn't he? I've seen the pictures. It was grim. There're always more victims than you think, isn't there? That poor bugger will probably never get over this."

Tanya glanced around. "It was everything though, the smell, the blue bottles, the head missing, it was really terrible for them. At the end of the day there are some people we can't help no matter how successful the enquiry is, not really part of it, but scarred for life. Let's go and have a word with his friend, Spencer. With luck, he'll be more together."

Chapter 23

By the time Ana reached the first set of houses and a short row of shops, the roads had become busier. So many people. For the past few months, she had seen nobody but the girls in the caravans, the men in the van, and then they had all been together in the big shed. They hadn't been allowed to talk, except on the journey to and from working, and then at night when they were alone.

The hustle and bustle was disorienting, frightening, and though her English was good, she found, in the panic, that she couldn't understand what was being said around her. There were buses, cars everywhere and so many white vans just like the one that took them to the factory. She peered at them, trying to see into the windows without walking too close to the kerb edge, trying to keep her head down and her eyes up. Trying to achieve the impossible. She bumped into a lamppost, spun away and lurched into the side of a woman who was holding the hands of two small children. "Oy, watch where you're going, stupid bitch."

"Sorry, sorry. I– sorry."

"Bloody foreigners, go back where you came from if you can't cope with a proper country. Stupid bloody woman. You could have hurt my kids. Bloody drugs, I'll bet you're drunk."

"Sorry." She scuttled away, past the shops and the little supermarket, past the bus stops and the cafes. She needed a phone, she needed to call her brother and warn them at home.

She couldn't see a little red phone box anywhere. She had an image in her mind of the ones in the magazines and even from the pictures on the walls of the cross-channel ferry. She had seen the one in Dover, outside the hotel, but nowhere on this busy street was there anything like that. She saw the posting boxes, but they were no help.

She stopped an elderly woman trundling along with a basket on wheels. The woman's eyes rounded with shock. She clutched her black shoulder bag closer to her body as she backed away towards the safety of the nearest shop.

"Sorry, sorry." Ana tried to dredge up a smile, she held up her hands in what she hoped was a gesture of submission. "Sorry, I just need a telephone. Do you know where is a telephone?"

The woman relaxed a little, glanced around her and then shook her head. "No, my dear. No, they don't have them on this road anymore. I haven't seen one for such a long time. We all have our mobiles now, don't we?" She pulled a small plastic handset from her pocket. "So much better. Those phone boxes were nasty, smelly places. Have you not got your mobile with you?"

Ana shook her head, hope flared for a moment as the woman glanced down at her own device. "Maybe I can borrow?" She pointed at the woman's Nokia.

"Oh, I don't know, I'm pay-as-you-go you know."

Ana had no idea what this meant but she did understand 'pay' and she had no money, a few coins in her purse left from her travelling money. She held them out to the woman.

"That's only about fifty pence dear. Where do you want to call, is it UK?"

"No, no, my brother. I need to call my brother in Bosnia."

"Oh my word, no, no – I can't let you do that. No." The woman shook her head and made to move away.

"Please, please. Could I send him a text, just a text that is all?"

"No, I'm sorry I don't know how much that would cost, I don't think I have the balance, I can't help you. No, you'll have to go to the pub or something. I think they might have a phone. I can't help you." She turned to walk away.

Ana panicking now, reached out to lay a hand on the woman's arm. "Please, where is pub? Please help me."

"Let go, let go. Stop it now. Leave me alone."

Ana didn't mean for the woman to fall, she had never intended to cause harm. Desperation made her grip the woman's arm tighter. As she pulled to try and escape, her feet tangled with the frame of her shopping bag, the handbag on her shoulder swung forward, and she began to lose her balance. Ana let go of her arm and reached out to steady her, but the result was just more screaming, more flurry.

"Help me, help me," she squealed.

As she fell, her head made brief contact with the edge of the trolley. Old, weak skin split, causing more screaming and now there was blood. There appeared to be a lot of blood and the old woman clutched at her chest and fell back against the dirty paving stones.

People had turned to look, a couple of women stepped from the doorway of the little supermarket. The situation was escalating. Ana wanted to call her brother, more than anything she wanted to save her family. She reached out and pulled the phone from the old hand. Tears had started to her eyes, she had no choice. She really had no choice. "Sorry. I am sorry."

She turned and ran, leaving a crowd gathering around the old woman. As she ran, she heard them begin to shout.

"Stop her, stop her. She's mugged this old woman. Somebody stop that girl."

Chapter 24

Finch offered to make Tanya a cup of coffee with the new machine. She wasn't going to cut off her nose to spite her face, and it did smell good. "Yeah, great thanks."

With the little white ceramic mugs in hand, they walked into the incident room. She was glad he hadn't given her a saucer; there were some on the table – she didn't even use them at home. She wasn't a slob, but this guy was something else, he really was.

The team gathered around. Everyone was present, including the half a dozen civilians who had been viewing the CCTV. It didn't go unnoticed that Sue Rollinson sidled up beside Finch. "Hmm, that coffee smells good," she said.

Tanya cringed quietly to herself. She thought that her talk a while ago had paid dividends when the detective constable had reeled in the inappropriate interest in Charlie Lambert, but apparently, it wasn't so. Tanya was irritated that the woman couldn't understand what a backward step this sort of thing was for women in the force. If they were seen as flirts and giggly girls, how could those who were serious about their careers ever break the glass ceiling? Okay, relationships developed, it was inevitable, and yes, there were women in high office now, the highest offices in fact, but this woman was a lurch back in time.

She really didn't have the time or patience for it, but it would feel disloyal to have the woman removed from the team. However, if it came to that, so be it. They all had to make their own choices and she could never say she hadn't been warned.

"Right, anything we need to know about?" She addressed the room at large. There was a general shaking of heads until one of the civilians spoke up.

"I'm not sure if it's anything and I don't have much but…"

"Yes?" Tanya said.

All eyes turned to the woman standing near the back of the group.

"Well, I've been looking at the road outside the entrance to the golf club. The CCTV takes in the car park and part of the road in both directions. It's a bit of a tricky junction so they like to monitor it. There have been a couple of bumps apparently. Anyway, there was a van, a white one that drove past three days before the body was discovered, late in the evening. It headed in the direction of the hut, on the other side of the hedge, you know?"

Tanya nodded. "Why were you interested, sorry I didn't catch your name?"

"Sylvia, ma'am, Sylvia Moon."

"Okay, so as I say, why were you alerted to this van?"

"Well, as it passed on the way towards the hut, I noticed that there was a rear light out and the number plate illumination was compromised. I couldn't make out the letters, neither front nor rear. I noted it and less than half an hour later the same van came back. There isn't anywhere around there that would explain such a short trip. No houses, no pub, nothing like that. So, either he was lost and had to do a u-turn or – well I suppose he could have been fly-tipping or something."

"Have you followed that up? Any reports of dumping around there?"

"No, ma'am. None reported."

Good work, Ms Moon. Has anyone else picked up this van? What was the make?"

"It was a VW, ma'am, transporter – white, not new."

Tanya waited for a while but although there was a lot of muttering, no one else came up with a sighting. "Right, back to the screens, let's see if we can find this van. Keep up with the questioning of golfers and fishermen and add a question about the VW with a rear light out, erm… right or left, Sylvia?"

"Left, ma'am."

"We didn't get very far with the questioning of the original witnesses today, but someone, somewhere has seen something and we need to ferret it out. Detective Constable Rollinson, you're with me, we've got the manager of the golf club coming in any time and I have a feeling about him."

Chapter 25

Ana ran from the yelling crowd and around the first corner. She tucked herself into the rear doorway of one of the shops.

Poking at the little buttons on the cheap handset, she could hear the click and whistle on the line. It was taking forever; time she didn't have. She stepped back and forth from her hiding place. Out in the road, there was more shouting and the thud of feet. She watched a group of teenagers dash across the end of the little alley, whooping and yelling.

She pressed back against the wall, her heart pounding, sick with fear. When two young men turned into the alley, pointed at her and charged to where she stood, there was nowhere to run. She dragged her bag from her shoulder, thrust it behind a rubbish skip and pulled a piece of metal in front of the gap. It was all she had in the world and she couldn't let them take it away.

They had her, trapped in the alley, pressed against the wet wall. A PCSO was passing, trying to calm the situation and find out just what had happened. She pushed forward, taking control.

Though Ana was saved from the men, she was held, not unkindly, but firmly while transport was called for. She was taken into custody with the shouts and jeers of the shoppers, the shopworkers, and the teens – none of whom she could understand – ringing in her ears.

The PCSO had taken the phone from her and shaken her head at the old, cheap device. "Really, you caused all that fuss, for this?"

Ana didn't answer, she was afraid to speak and afraid to let them know she was not English, though surely they could tell. She was afraid of what they would ask her. If things had been bad for her family before, then when she was with the police, things would be worse, much worse.

She tried to see how this could be a good thing. If she told them what had happened, how she had been kept, how the others were being held – locked in the old house, short of food, no proper facilities, sleeping on mattresses on the floor – maybe the British police would help them.

But what if they made her go back? What if they made her show them the caravan and the house? Then everyone would know it was her. Maybe the way they were being kept wasn't illegal here in this country. She had no rights, she'd been told that. They couldn't go to the police or complain to anyone at the factory because they had no rights. They had signed a contract with the agency back at home, handing over all responsibility, and that was all they had.

Now they must do as they were told and work to pay for their expenses and only then would applications be made for their documents. Only after that would they be legal. As time had gone on, she had seen this for the lie that it was. By that time, it was too late to do anything about it. She was involved with all the others, and their fates were entangled. Now, bundled into a blue van and taken to the police station, she was frightened into total silence. She didn't know who it would be safe to speak to, and there was no one to help her. They were polite, they didn't beat her or strip her, as she thought they might. They left her alone in a small, bare room with a table, three chairs, some electrical equipment against the wall, and with a cup of tea in a plastic cup in front of her. The door was locked, and she was alone except for a silent young man in uniform who seemed embarrassed to look at her.

Chapter 26

Steven Traynor had been shown into an interview room; they kept him waiting, winding up the tension.

"What the hell is this about now? Why have I been brought down here?"

He was angry… she wanted him angry. Angry people spoke carelessly.

"Mr Traynor." Tanya placed a thin file folder on the table in front of her. "You're free to leave at any time, you do understand that?"

He glared at her. "I've answered your questions. I have nothing to do with that body. I was as shocked as everyone else about all that. What the hell." He stopped and began gnawing at the skin around his thumbnail.

Tanya flicked open the file. The crime scene images were horrible. If she showed him, then he would have them imprinted forever in his mind. On the other hand, if he was guilty of anything to do with the murder, then he may already have a good idea of what the inside of the hut had looked like. She shifted the folder in front of her, spun it on the table top and laid two separate images side by side.

He glanced at them briefly, gave a strangled gasp, covered his mouth with his hand and screwed his eyes tightly shut. "Shit, what the hell. Put it away, Christ." He opened his eyes now but turned his head so that he didn't have to look at the pictures.

Tanya slid the papers together, flipped the cover closed and laid a hand on top of the file.

"I didn't need to see that. Bloody hell. That's enough. I'm leaving. I'm going to the papers about this. You've no right. No right to do that," he snarled.

"I'm sorry, Mr Traynor., I know the images are distressing – they are distressing for all of us. I would like you to have a look. It's possible you might recognise something, the build of our victim for example. Could you just have a look?"

He pushed his chair away from the table. It tipped and clattered backwards onto the tiled floor. The constable standing near the door stepped forward. Tanya held up her hand.

"No, I won't bloody look at it. What are you playing at?"

"We're in the middle of a serious enquiry. I would have thought you'd want to help, want to do anything that helps to move things along."

"Of course I bloody do, but no, not that. I don't want to see, that." He pointed a quivering finger towards the table. "I can't be asked to look at that."

"Okay." She pulled the file closer.

Sue Rollinson picked up the chair and stood beside it while he lowered himself back to the seat.

"I apologise if you found that distressing. Perhaps you could just go over some details for us. Do you want a drink, a glass of water?"

He shook his head but pulled the chair nearer to the table. Now that she had covered the images, she had brought him over to her side. Taking away the cause of upset made him feel that she had done him a favour. He was breathing more steadily. He had calmed down and leaned a little towards her.

Again, they went over the staffing of the club and the events of the week leading up to the discovery. All things they already knew but done on the off chance he had remembered something else or in case they could pick up on anomalies or contradictions. She assured him that they were re-visiting all the witnesses. He would know that anyway because she was sure, though the course itself was off limits, the bar and clubhouse were not, and gossip would be rife.

After another half an hour she stood and held out her hand. "Well thanks so much for coming in, Mr Traynor. I'm sorry for the inconvenience and really do apologise for the unpleasantness."

He touched her outstretched fingers briefly. "Well, I hope that's the end of it."

"I wish it was, but we are still working to find out just what happened, so I can't make any promises."

"Oh yes, of course. Well, I realise that, don't I? What I meant was the end of dragging me down here, asking questions and more questions about things we've already gone over, and that." He pointed at the file. "I never want to see anything like that again."

"He seemed really rattled, didn't he?" Sue said as they walked back up the stairs and down the corridor to the incident room. "He was completely shaken. I don't think he had any idea."

"Well, either that or he's a bloody good actor. But no, I think you're right. They are pretty gruesome." Tanya lifted the hand holding the folder. "If he'd seen it before I don't think his reaction would have been quite so strong. I don't know though, Sue. I still think there's something off about him. It's just a feeling."

Chapter 27

Tanya stared at the printout. In the other corner of the office, she could hear the click of Brian Finch's mouse and the occasional clatter of his keyboard. On top of everything else, the bloody man was a touch typist. He could have his reports and emails accurately finished before Tanya had put together a few paragraphs. She glanced up. Was there nothing that he wasn't brilliant at?

He had taken over the briefing while she had interviewed Traynor. He had followed that up by fielding an anxious call from DCI Scunthorpe who needed something to tell the Chief Constable. He had received complaints from 'friends' who were champing at the bit not being able to play golf. He had smoothed the ruffled feathers without committing the team to anything impossible to achieve.

When she came back into the room, irritated and frustrated, it was to find the team at their desks and monitors, the board updated, and the DI in conversation with Dan Price, who was chatting happily, sharing a laugh, something she had rarely seen from the shy and diffident detective constable. He obviously had a knack with people, on top of everything else.

"Have you seen this, Brian?" She waved the A4 sheet at him.

"Yes, I've got it here on my tablet. She was pretty."

"Hmm." Tanya looked at the dark-haired woman. They had given her brown eyes, in keeping with the tone of her skin and hair. But the artist stressed they could be off with that, they could have been green, hazel or even blue and there was no way to tell. When the DNA results came back, they would have a better idea. She had a heart-shaped face, a wide mouth and a small, straight nose. She was indeed pretty, and they had photoshopped her long curling hair, so different from the bedraggled rat's tails Tanya remembered. With the sheen on her curls and the light in her eyes, she looked alive, real, and heartbreakingly hopeful staring out from the image. Had they deliberately given her face that expression? Maybe so – hoping it would make people more likely to sympathise, keener to want to help.

"It's going on the news bulletins, the rolling twenty-four hour and the regional. We are putting up posters, and we've got bods on the ground, doing door to door in the nearest houses. Not that there are that many. I don't know, Brian. If you had a head and hands in a bag you wouldn't get rid close to home, would you?" Tanya said.

"Probably not, no."

"So, are we looking at two crimes, completely separate? In which case we have to put the call out nationwide. Kate Lewis has been updating HOLMES already and looking at the posts. She's trying for matches and we've got to hope for the best there. We need to find out if there is anyone with a body and no head; come to that, we need to find if there is anyone with a head, hands and no body. In reality, though, they've got to be related, haven't they? I mean what are the chances of two murders, two dismembered corpses in such close proximity?"

"Seems rather unlikely. What do you reckon about this van?" Brian said.

Tanya shrugged. "A van, a white van. I wonder just how many thousands there are in this area alone. It could have been anything, a perfectly innocent punter lost, a courting couple looking for somewhere quiet to have sex. It could have been one of so many different things."

"And, yet, the number plate was obscured, it was in the right area, and it's all we've got."

Tanya lowered her head to the desk. "You're right. Shit. Anyway, it's getting late. No point hanging around now. I'm going to go home and get my occurrence book in order, go through everything again, away from the phones and what have you, and look for a thread to pull. I'm going to have fingers and toes crossed that something comes of this." She waved the picture again. "There are plenty of people manning the phones and I've asked the team to hang on for a while, just a couple of hours and then back in the morning early."

"Right, I think I'll stick around for a while, help with the calls just in case anything interesting comes in," Brian said.

She stared at him for a minute. Now he'd made her feel like a slacker. She had sat up half the night going over it and over it and knew that tonight would be the same, but he made her feel that she was skiving.

"I'll call you straight away if there's anything you need to know about. You look done in."

He'd left her no choice now but to leave him to it, if she changed her mind, she'd look flaky. Bugger the man, he was really getting under her skin.

Chapter 28

Cheese on toast and a glass of whisky was Tanya's choice of comfort food. She ate the stodgy, greasy snack and enjoyed the fire in her throat from the single malt. Something would click soon; she just had to keep going.

The house was quiet, and she remembered just how much she used to like that. However, it was strange getting used to it again. The discovery of the body, getting back to full-time work, had coincided with Serena leaving. Perhaps that was why it was hard to adjust – too many changes on top of each other.

Surely, this was good; it was what she wanted.

She couldn't shake the sense of foreboding though. Finch was unsettling her, and not for the first time she wished for Charlie back. As if he knew, the mobile rang and his ID flashed onto the screen.

"Hiya. How are you?" she said.

"I'm good thanks, great. You?"

They went through the preliminaries. Carol was getting better all the time and it seemed that she was emerging from the fug of postnatal depression. Joshua was trying to walk and was already talking. Tanya made the appropriate responses, but when he asked her how she was feeling, she couldn't speak. Her throat had closed. She coughed. *What the hell was that?*

"Actually, I'm fine, thanks. Busy, really pushed at work." She gave him an outline of the cases and they tossed a few ideas around. It was good to remember what it used to be like.

It was Charlie who changed the subject. "How's Serena? Still driving you mad with her music? Have you sorted out college for her?"

"Actually no. She's gone back to her mum."

As she spoke, Tanya felt awkward and embarrassed, as though she had something to be ashamed of. His reaction didn't help. Silence followed by a non-committal grunt.

She filled the space. "It's for the best. She needs to be with her family."

"Well, you're family," he said, "and at least you're calmer than your dibby sister. I thought it was a good idea, her being with you for a while. Until she got over everything. I know she didn't remember much about it, but gang rape isn't something you're ever going to be able to accept. It's very early days. That's what family is for, isn't it? You know, helping each other."

"Yeah, well she's gone."

He caught the tone and changed the subject, but Tanya reached out for her glass and took a big gulp of whisky.

"So, how are the team? It must be great for you to have them all together on this new case. Well, cases as it turns out."

"Yeah, it's good. Everyone's fine. Bloody Sue is up to her old tricks though." She winced as she spoke. Of course, it had been Charlie that Sue had set her sights on. She didn't know how he would feel being reminded. In the event he was typical Charlie.

"She's a predator that one. It's a shame because she's got the makings of a good detective, but she's not going to go the distance, is she? I reckon she'll snag a man and that'll be that – career stalled. Pity. Anyway, who is she stalking now, not Dan?" He laughed.

"No, we've got a new bloke. A new DI actually."

"Oh right, my replacement."

"Ha, you know they can't replace you, Charlie." Tanya's mood lifted as she heard him chuckle.

"Well, of course not. No, come on, who is it, do I know him?"

"Brian Finch. About your age, I guess. A bit dapper, seems pretty clued up. Computer whizz, apparently, though he hasn't been tested on that yet. We've got so little to go on, there's been nothing to compute."

"Ah. Finch. Tall, dark-haired, good looking."

"I guess."

"He was just behind me at Hendon," Charlie said

"So, did you know him at all?"

"Not so much. He's from a different background and he wasn't on my course anyway. Family's rolling in it apparently. Father's a banker I think, mother's something legal, a solicitor or maybe even a silk. I remember him being fast-tracked and sent off for computer courses. Oh yes, and there's an uncle – an ACC somewhere – I think that's why I remember him."

"He seems very… capable." Tanya struggled to find the right word.

There was a silence, she could hear him breathing. "Look, Tanya, you know what it's like in places like the college, and I don't know anything specific but …"

"What?"

"Well, just watch your back, you know."

"Charlie, come on. You can't say that and leave me hanging. What the hell do you mean?"

"No, I won't repeat rumours and gossip, anyway people change, mature and what have you. But you're my mate so, well as I say, just watch your back. Look, I need to go, Carol's out and the baby's crying. I'll ring again soon. You should come up and see us. I think you'd like Liverpool, it's buzzin'."

"Just before you go though, Charlie. I wonder if you could do me a favour?"

"Course I will. If I can."

"It's just you mentioning Liverpool. Can you have a root around, see if there is any mention of a bloke called – hang on – ah! Mulholland, first name Jamie? See if anyone recognises the name or whatever. I think he's from up there. Young, probably about late twenties, dark blonde hair, fit; not sure I can tell you much more. Hm… it's not much, is it? That's what this bloody case is like."

"What are you looking for?"

"Well, nothing specific, it's just that it was mentioned he was from up there. He works at the golf club, you know, where we found the first body. I don't feel happy about the manager and… well, just 'no tern unstoned' as they say."

She heard him laugh again. "Yeah, okay got that – I'll let you know. Take care, Tanya."

"And you, Charlie. Say hi to Carol. I'm glad she's getting better." And he was gone, the night was quieter and the strange feeling of something like loneliness deeper. She shook her head, logged out of the computer and went to bed.

Chapter 29

Ana wouldn't speak; not at all. When the PCSO couldn't make any progress, they brought in a more experienced female officer to talk quietly and gently; then a young man, and then an older man who they thought might seem a father figure. Nobody could break through the barrier. They told her there was no need to be afraid, tried several different languages; dredged the whole of the station for anyone who could put a sentence together in anything other than English. But she said not a word. She cried, constantly and silently, dabbing at her face with a succession of crumpled tissues. She shook her head, but she did not speak.

In the end they had no option but to take her to the cells which meant they had to go through the whole routine, take DNA samples, fingerprints and photographs.

"It's bloody ridiculous," the custody sergeant grumbled, "it's an ancient old phone, it makes no sense."

"I know, but the old biddy's got stitches in her head and is suffering from shock. They're keeping her in for observation," the PCSO told him. "Well, she is knocking on a bit and you can't be too careful. From what I've gathered, it wasn't much more than a bit of a push and shove resulting in an accident, but she wants to make a fuss. Says she can't remember any of the conversation because she was so frightened. She's old so it's not that surprising but she has confirmed the girl's a foreigner. Said that she wanted to ring home and it was one of those countries with a funny name, Arab she thought. She said that she had nothing against foreigners but maybe they'd be happier if they went home. No prejudice there then. I think the old woman is enjoying the attention. This poor girl seems more upset."

"Yes, I know, Karen, but we're stuck. She had nothing on her, no identification, nothing, so until she decides to speak to us, we can't do anything more than we have. We've called the doctor, but she's not physically hurt, so he's not rushing. Could be ages, and I think we'll have to bring in a psychologist if we can, make sure there's nothing wrong with her, you know." He made a circle with his fingers a couple of inches from the side of his forehead. "Waste of time and money, but it's looking as though she might have to answer to a charge of assault."

Before she went back to the streets the PCSO peered into the cell where Ana was curled in a ball on the thin blue mattress. Her eyes were closed, her arms wrapped tightly around her body and it was clear that she was still crying. She lifted a finger to her face and wiped away the tears.

Karen Laidlaw turned away and admitted to herself that she wished she'd let the poor woman go. She'd learn from this. Sticking to the rules was great but sometimes just keeping things simple was a better bet. She felt guilty, which was ridiculous really because she'd done the right thing.

Back on the high street, the drama was already forgotten, the hue and cry no more than something to laugh about in the betting office.

Karen went back to the alleyway; back to the dirty doorway. There was not much here beside dog shit and empty bottles, and a couple of discarded needles. She kicked at the door, but it was locked. She hoisted herself onto the top of the wall with her hands and saw nothing but ancient debris and dirty puddles in a depressing back yard.

Behind the wheelie bin she found the cheap plastic shoulder bag. She took it into the road, where there was more light and less stink. She knew before she looked inside what it was. There was no point going over the top, calling in crime scene officers or stuffing it into an evidence bag – this was all about a crappy old phone really. She pulled open the zip. There wasn't much inside, some clothes, mostly clean but worn, some tissues and bits of makeup, and a plastic folder holding four photographs. Three were of individuals and the fourth was a group shot. Karen didn't know where it was taken but it was obviously not England. She reckoned Eastern Europe from the few buildings that were visible. In the middle of the group was the girl she had arrested earlier. There was nothing written on the back but at least they had a start.

She trekked back to the station and presented the bag to the custody sergeant. It was frustrating to leave it with him. She wanted to take the picture in to the girl to see if she could get her to speak now and let her know that her stuff was safe.

"Let me know what happens, will you?" she asked.

"Aye, I will. Well done, lass. This'll be a big help."

Chapter 30

"Brian. Yeah." As she answered the phone, rubbing at her face with the other hand, Tanya was surprised to see pale light leaking in through the bedroom blind. She didn't feel she had slept well, she'd had vivid and disturbing dreams, but at quarter to seven, it was much later than she thought.

"Sorry to disturb you," Brian said.

"It's okay, I was up." Okay, it was a lie, but as she spoke, she swung her legs out from under the duvet. "What's going on?"

"I'm out near Duke's Cut."

"Oh right. Something happened?" she asked.

"We've found a body. In the woods, on the other side of the A40."

She was fully awake now, already reaching for her jeans and sweatshirt. "Why didn't dispatch call me?"

It didn't matter really, but it was the first question that came to mind, and she had blurted it out. "Anyway, never mind about that for now. Wait though, just hang on."

He had caught her unprepared and now she was flustered. There was a pen on her bedside table, a notepad, and she perched on the edge of the mattress and took a deep breath. She closed her eyes for a moment and tried again. "Right, sorry. Exactly, where are you, and what details do we have?"

"I'm at Oxey Mead Lake, the other side of the A40 from Duke's Cut. There are more woods, more small lakes."

"Who found the body?" She had laid her phone on the cabinet, switched it to speaker, and was dragging on her clothes one handed while trying to jot down relevant details. She knew it was ridiculous, what she should do was take the call quietly and calmly, but she felt wrong footed.

"Jogger. I suppose we would have got to it eventually, by widening the search around Duke's Cut, but anyway, here it is," Brian said.

"Have you had sight of it?" she asked.

"I have. It's a female, naked. I think it's been here a few days – there's evidence of wildlife."

"Ah, so – head, or no head?"

"No, no head, no hands."

"I'm on my way, we need to get things in motion. I'll call the Medical Examiner, the SOCO team," Tanya said.

"Yeah, I've got that in place, they should be here within the next ten minutes or so."

She hesitated, she had to be calm. "Right. Well, I'll see you there."

She clicked off the phone, and finished dressing, grabbed a bottle of water and a breakfast bar from the cupboard, and was in her car minutes later.

She was seething with anger and confusion. In the back of her mind, she re-ran Charlie's words. *"Watch your back."* She was SIO, she should have been called first. But surely there was a logical explanation for what had happened. Using the hands-free she interrogated the missed calls list. Nothing. At least that was something – she hadn't slept through them trying to reach her. But in that case, why had they not called? She turned onto the main road, the tyres singing in the early morning damp, the sun painting wet roofs a dull pink, and she struggled to get her mind into

the right place. The main thing was this body, the rest of it
would have to be dealt with; later, and calmly. But it would
be dealt with.

Chapter 31

By the time Tanya arrived the full circus was underway –
tents and tapes, cars, vans, and dogs. A constable standing
guard at a small iron gate noted her name and told her to
stick to the safe path, pointing down at the metal walkway
that had already been laid. She was irritated he felt she
needed to be told, but he was just doing his job and doing
it well. It wasn't him really, she was just generally irritated.

Paper suited, and with a pair of bootees covering her
own shoes, she stepped carefully along the slippery path.
The undergrowth was wet, the surroundings muddy.
Maybe that would help, there could be footprints in the
soft ground. As she walked, she took it all in. Part of her
mind was back in that other area of woodland, to the first
ever murder victim she had seen. There had been birdsong
that time, and trees and shrubs, and just as now, there had
been horror.

She dipped into the blue tent. Simon Hewitt was there,
bending over the corpse, dictating quietly into his machine.
The flare of camera flash bounced off the plastic walls and
threw the sad remains into stark relief against grass made
lurid by artificial light. There was no head, and the arms
ended in dirty stumps. The body lay on its back, pale and

sad. Female for certain and not very old but rendered inhuman by the twisted pose and the missing extremities.

The victim's left breast had been torn and ruined by a bullet, the hole darkened around the edges. Dr Hewitt saw her and raised a hand. "We've got a cause of death at least," he said. "From the evidence of liver mortice and lack of blood here" – he swept a hand around him – "I would say that she has been moved after death. I have turned her, there is an exit wound in the back. So, while we can see what happened to the poor thing, we are not much further on finding out where, or indeed, why. It makes me wonder now about the body on the golf course. Indications there would be that the injury was to the head, maybe another bullet, but until we find it…" He shrugged.

She glanced around; everyone was busy. She would read the reports when they came in, would attend the post-mortem examination herself, but right now she was nothing more than an onlooker and a latecomer. A spectator.

Back in the clearing, Brian Finch was addressing a group of uniformed officers, instructing them as to areas to be searched, giving them enough background so they knew what they might be looking for.

"I suppose we're looking for the head?"

Tanya didn't see which one of them had spoken.

"No. We've got that, it was found earlier. We have no weapon though, no gun and nothing that would have been used to remove the head and hands," Finch said

Tanya walked across to stand beside him.

"Ah, right. Detective Inspector Miller is SIO," he said. "I'm just briefing the search team, boss. Getting things going."

"Yes, I heard."

She waited a moment until she had their attention. "Actually, we are looking for a head, guys."

She heard him huff beside her, knew that she was being petty but couldn't help herself. "Not this one, as it happens," she continued, "but we have another body. It's possibly all part of the same crime, we don't know for certain yet. That was a male. I recognise some of you who were over there at the golf club."

A few of the group nodded and mumbled.

"Well, we still don't have the head and hands from that poor bloke, so…" She glanced at Brian Finch. "In answer to the question, yes, you need to be aware that there could be a head, maybe hands. Possibly in a sack. Okay, off you go."

She watched them step carefully into the surrounding undergrowth before she spoke again. "I think we have to organise a dive team for these ponds." She indicated two more stretches of water, and from the glint beyond the trees, a smaller one some way off.

"I've put in the call," Finch said.

She glared up at him, sighed. "Right well, I'd better get on to the DCI, he'll need to authorise the expenditure."

"I had a word earlier."

"When earlier?"

"Just before I called you."

Anger began to build, she tamped it down, spoke calmly. "Bit arse about face, wasn't it? I would have thought your first call would have been to me."

"Sorry, I just thought I might as well get things moving. Bob's cleared the dive team anyway."

She noted the use of the DCI's first name. Was it to let her know there was closer contact between them than simply being colleagues? If so, it was totally unprofessional.

"How come you were first on scene, Brian? I checked my phone, I didn't miss any calls."

"I had a word with dispatch, yesterday, after you left. Just made them aware that I was first contact, with you going off home. I was trying to let you get some rest. The stupid sods must have thought I meant continually, you know, not just for yesterday evening. Oh yes, that reminds me. Nothing as yet from the image. I hung around until midnight, helping with the phones and keeping an eye on things. Just the usual stuff, people who thought they'd seen the dead woman shopping in Tesco and what not."

She didn't trust herself to speak. There was no reasonable response that wouldn't sound defensive. She turned away. "I'll see you back at the station. Call in the team, would you?"

"Yeah. I did that. They should be there by the time we get back."

Chapter 32

"I think in future, to avoid duplication and confusion it would be best if you let me know about any major developments. You know, before you get into the nitty-gritty of arranging to call in SOCO, the medical examiner, and the rest of it, oh yes, and calling the DCI." Tanya was walking a tightrope between sounding professional and factual and allowing her pique and annoyance to bleed through.

"Yeah, fine. I just thought I might as well get things moving, you know. We haven't made a lot of progress up to now, so I didn't think we should waste time standing on ceremony." Finch's stare was unblinking and smug. He had the upper hand. He hadn't done anything wrong, but they both knew he had been subversive.

Tanya could give him a speech about being a team player, watching out for who you stood on while you climbed the ladder, and professional consideration, but really, she wasn't the one to do it. She had always found working with others challenging but she knew that she had never done anything quite so blatantly self-serving.

"Well anyway, as you say, the main thing is to keep things moving. I'm going to the post-mortem. I think it would be great if you could collate the reports from last night, seeing as you were so much more involved. I imagine by now there is quite a heap of calls to sort through. If you find anything that looks promising just let me know, eh? If you want to go out and speak to any of the callers, let Kate know where you're going, in case I need you urgently. I'll take Sue Rollinson with me to the morgue."

It was a small victory, barely more than an irritation to him, but there wasn't really any way that he could squirm out of it. Not after making such a fuss about staying late to help man the phones. She stuck her head round the incident room door to collect Sue, and as she walked along the corridor, heading for the car park, a small smile crept across her face.

* * *

"Tanya." Simon Hewitt smiled at her from his position behind the cutting table. "I thought for a while there that you'd left us."

"Sorry?" Tanya shook her head. "Not sure what you mean."

"When the other chap turned up this morning, introduced himself as an inspector. That's new isn't it?"

"Oh right, yes. His promotion has just come through."

"Well anyway, it's good to see that you're still with us," he said.

Tanya felt Sue Rollinson's eyes on her. She had long thought that Dr Hewitt had a bit of a thing for Tanya, and had been responsible for rumours and innuendo.

Looking at him now, his grey eyes twinkling, Tanya had to admit that it wouldn't be the worst thing in the world. He had once suggested that they meet up away from the pressures of work, but she'd missed it. She had been so wrapped up in her examination of a murder victim that it had taken Rollinson to tell her it had happened. It had been so embarrassing that she'd avoided being on her own with him since then, but today she felt in need of a friend. "Yes, well it's good to be working with you, Simon, it really is." She was rewarded with a beaming smile as he picked up his knife.

"Right, if we're ready, let's have a look at what we've got here."

He paused for a moment, closed his eyes, and stood silently beside the corpse. She had seen him do this before, she didn't know whether he was praying or simply giving the person in front of him respect and a moment of sympathy. It was moving and it impacted on them all – there was silence in the cold, tiled room.

He lifted his head and without another word he reached forward and began the Y incision, the cuts reaching from shoulder to shoulder and meeting at the breastbone.

Chapter 33

Kate Lewis had updated the boards and the team were still fielding calls about the pictures of the young woman's face. It had been on the early bulletins and in the morning papers. "Anything?" Tanya asked.

Dan Price raised his hand. "It's not from the victim image, ma'am, but I have something here from the golf course."

"Right, well you might as well share it with all of us straight away."

She could have let him come and tell her quietly in the office. She knew that he would have preferred it, but he was going to have to toughen up. He was a good detective, but he would never get anywhere if he couldn't handle a team. She wanted them all to do well. It wasn't her place to stand in their way and it was inconceivable to her that they would accept failure. He was blushing furiously, and she wondered how he had ever managed to deal with members of the public when he'd been in uniform.

"We have some CCTV of a white van at the golf course," he said.

"The same white van?"

Hope soared, but he shook his head.

"Not possible to be sure. It's the same make, looks to be about the same age but there are no distinguishing marks, nothing like that."

"The registration?" Tanya asked.

"Sorry, ma'am. The thing is, the cameras are set up to watch the junction and he came from behind. Could be the driver knew that, of course."

"What was it doing? I'll look at the vid myself of course, but just give us a rundown, would you?"

"Well again, we don't have much. It entered the carpark then pulled around the side of the clubhouse. We could see that the rear doors were open for a while. Unfortunately, we couldn't see exactly what was happening. The view was obscured by the building. Sorry, ma'am, it's not very much, is it?"

Tanya had to admit that it wasn't.

"Watch it again, I'll come and have a look. See if they can get us a decent view of the driver. I'll leave that with you, chase them until you've got anything at all – there must be something they can do, he was inside after all. Just gender, hopefully, skin colour, an indication of age. Challenge them, they're egotistical bastards in the tech department, needle 'em a bit, Dan." She knew that she was torturing him, but she needed more. "We need to find this van," she said.

"The report from Dr Hewitt will be a couple of hours, but at least we know the cause of death. We know that the body was moved and though he hasn't confirmed it yet, he is pretty convinced that the head and hands are a match for this body. It's coming together guys, slowly I know, but every bit is a step nearer. We'll do this. We just need to keep going," Tanya said to the team.

She had never been one for encouraging speeches but, right now, she needed them on her side; needed to remind them who was in charge. She was rewarded by smiles from Kate and Dan Price, and even Paul Harris gave her a nod of acknowledgement.

"DI Finch, I think we'll go back to the golf club again, as soon as we've seen the video. Get me a couple of stills of the truck would you, Kate?"

"We could just take the video on my iPhone." Finch had taken the handset from his pocket and waved it in the air.

"Yeah, fine." Tanya glanced at him. "I think we'll take some stills though, Kate. Easier to put in front of witnesses in my experience."

This was becoming more and more petty and difficult. She would have to go and speak to Bob Scunthorpe. Now that his promotion had been confirmed, surely they could move Finch on to something else. It was bad enough trailing through the mire in this case without him second guessing her decisions and trying to score points. She went into the office and closed the door behind her. "Shit, Charlie," she muttered, "why the hell did you have to bugger off to bloody Liverpool?"

The door opened and Finch stomped in, tense and angry. He went to his coffee machine and stuck a pod into the slot.

Tanya smiled to herself – there wasn't going to be an espresso for her.

Chapter 34

"Afternoon, Karen." The custody sergeant nodded at the young PCSO. "Still can't let it go, eh?"

She shook her head. "Any progress, Sarge?"

"I suppose you could call it that. We've managed to convince the old woman that there's no point in the waste of money and time trying to get a conviction over her cheap little phone. She was hurt, I know, but when we questioned her, she admitted that she fell more than was pushed. More than anything she was looking for a bit of fuss really but she still can't remember much of what was said. Anyway, we've allocated her a victim support officer and it seems to have been enough. I don't think she can really face the thought of court and lawyers and all of that. She's got her phone back, so that part of it is all about settled."

"And the girl?"

"Well, it's pretty clear what it's all about, isn't it? She still won't talk to anyone, but we've contacted immigration. They've got experts who usually manage to get through to these poor sods. We're trying to find out where she entered the country, ports and what not, assuming she came in through one of them and not on a dinghy across the channel. Eventually, she'll give it up, she has to, and then more than likely she'll just be given a caution and be sent home, wherever that might be."

"Has she been given her photographs?" Karen asked.

"No, we showed them to her. There were tears, as you would expect, but we're holding them back for now. She'll be given all her stuff in due course, but they're the only thing we've got that she has really reacted to. Poor bloody woman. You know, I've got a daughter about the same age; makes you think, doesn't it?"

"When will she be transferred, do you know?"

"We have to get clearance from the CPS that there aren't going to be any charges, and then we need to get her taken away. We can't just let her loose, not if she won't prove she's here legally, and with no passport, well..." He shrugged. "They are trying to find some sort of accommodation until her fate is decided. Hopefully, we'll be rid of her sometime this afternoon, or possibly tomorrow morning. Depends on when they can send for her."

"Can you let me know? I'd like to, oh I don't know, just say goodbye or something."

"You can't let them get to you. Not like this." He looked into Karen's eyes, sad and hopeful. "Oh, go on then. I'll let you know. They won't let you go with her, you know."

"No, but I just thought a familiar face might make it all less scary."

"Aye, alright then. You'd better bugger off in the meantime and do some work."

"Yes, Sarge. Thanks."

* * *

Steven Traynor tried his best to be antagonistic and confrontational. His bitten finger nails, the outbreak of eczema on the back of his hands, and around his neck where his collar rubbed, spoiled the image of a controlling and annoyed club official.

Tanya told him that he could open the course again. The small wooden hut was however still out of bounds.

"Nobody will want to go in there anyway," he growled. "We're going to have it pulled down, going to burn the wood and dig up the area."

"You do realise that you will have to wait until we give you the okay, don't you?" Tanya said.

"Well, bloody obvious that, isn't it? If that's all, I have stuff to attend to. We're having a meeting of the committee to see how we are going to deal with the PR backlash. Have you seen the bloody newspapers? We need to attract new members. That's not happening, not with us being christened the Course of Horror and all the other stupid bloody stuff."

"Well, I'm afraid there's not much we can do about that. I would advise that you keep your contact with the press to a minimum, that way the interest will wane more quickly, in my experience," Tanya said.

"Well, as I say, it's a major problem for me right now, so…" He began to raise himself from his chair.

"There is one more thing, I'm afraid."

He lowered himself with an exaggerated sigh. "Yes?"

"We need a record of your deliveries, over the last three weeks."

"Deliveries?"

"Yes, the companies that you receive things from, times of receipt, the type of goods, you know, just details. The type of vehicle used, anything really that might help us."

He clasped his hands tightly together on the desk; they were shaking. She wondered if it was anger or something else, something more sinister. Tanya pressed home the advantage.

"What we're looking for really is a white van. A VW, a few years old, no company markings. It was picked up on the CCTV and we think it could be of interest. Does that ring any bells with you?"

"No, no – I don't deal with that stuff. The bar manager sees to all of that."

"What, everything?" she asked.

"Pretty much. There is some stuff for the pro shop but that's run as a sort of subsidiary by one of the big sports companies. They are only open three days a week. You'd have to speak to them."

"No, that's not it, I don't think. This was at the clubhouse, we reckon," Tanya said.

"Oh well, you'd have to speak to Jamie; he handles that, as I say."

"Could you maybe call him in for us?"

"What. Oh, no, he's off. You can't see him today."

"In that case, we need his address," said Finch. He had been silent up until this brief interjection. Steven Traynor glanced from one to the other.

"He hasn't done anything. I can't think why you want to bother him. I don't know whether I can give you his address – data protection and all that – and you must have taken it already, mustn't you? So that's harassment, probably."

Brian Finch leaned across the desk, Traynor's chair moved backwards on its casters.

"This is a murder enquiry. That means that if we ask you for something, you give it to us. Is there something there that you don't understand, Mr Traynor?" Finch said.

"The personnel files are in the cabinet." Traynor pointed to a set of metal drawers in the corner of the room.

"Excellent. If you would?" Finch said.

They didn't see it coming. They heard his breath quicken, watched as he paled, but when he cried out and grabbed at his chest it took them a moment to realise what was happening. It wasn't until he slumped to the floor that they reacted.

"Shit, call an ambulance!" Tanya ran around the desk and leaned down to lay fingers against Steven Traynor's neck. "Oh, bloody hell. There was a defibrillator in the club room, go and get it, Brian. Hurry up. Shift!" She turned Traynor onto his back and began to pump at his chest.

"Oh, you sod, you sod. Don't you dare do this, have you any bloody idea of the paperwork?"

Chapter 35

By the time the first responders arrived, Steven Traynor's heart was beating again. There was a feeble, thready pulse in his neck. His colour was terrible though, and there was no sign of him regaining consciousness. The paramedics congratulated Tanya. "If he survives this, it'll all be down to you," they said. But when she asked what his chances were, they shrugged and shook their heads, mouths turned down in the, *well it's not looking good,* expression she had expected.

Someone had to go to his home, notify his wife, and take her to the hospital. Tanya knew that if she did that she would be stuck there, waiting for a uniformed WPC so they could play pass the parcel with the woman who would no doubt be distraught. Surely it was better to send a patrol car in the first place. Best idea was for it to be an officer who could deliver the news, accompany the wife, and then sit and wait until they found out whether or not he would live. She made the call while Brian Finch searched in the filing cabinet for the personnel file of Jamie Mulholland.

"I don't suppose we can take this with us?" he said.

"Not without a warrant; probably shouldn't really be looking. Just get some pictures, will you?"

There was nothing much in the file, a date showing the start of his employment two years earlier. There was a couple of casual, handwritten references, most likely from friends – the letters were on plain paper, no letterheads, no official stamps. His NI number was there, and Tanya texted it through to Charlie along with a previous address in Kirkby on Merseyside.

He sent back a smiley face.

Back at the police station, they gave her a round of applause as she entered the incident room. "Good going, ma'am." Kate gave her a thumbs up. "I know we're supposed to know how to use a defib, but I'm not sure I'd have the nerve. Well, what I mean is, it's basically electrocuting someone isn't it."

"It was easy to use, Kate. The machine talks to you. It tells you exactly what to do. To be honest, we had nothing to lose, he was pretty much dead. Anyway, it's not looking good – he's in intensive care, apparently critical. I have a feeling he's not going to make it."

She threw her jacket across the back of a chair and stood beside the notice board. "DI Finch and I went to Jamie Mulholland's address. It's a flat, there was nobody home. We've left a message for him to call us, soon as. His phone goes right to voicemail, again I left a message. But it's only one line of enquiry. Traynor's reaction to questioning notwithstanding, we have no real proof that the bloke has done anything wrong. We mustn't lose sight of the fact that this crime could actually be nothing to do with the golf club." She held up her hand to quiet the murmur of comment. "It's possible that they have become involved, I guess you could say, by accident. It was a convenient place to dump a body and nothing more.

"Any luck with the white van yet?" She glanced around the room.

"We've had the view of the driver's face enhanced," Kate Lewis said.

"Well?"

"A couple of us think that it could be that bar manager. But it's not conclusive, just the size really and something about the way he moves. Youngish, you know. Fit. Of course, we might be seeing that because we want it to be him. Especially now that we know he's vanished." She shrugged, acknowledging that it was weak.

"Right, so it's been a different sort of a day." A couple of them laughed quietly. "But at the end of it, we are no further along. I'm open to suggestions, but I reckon we are going to have to go over old ground again – see what we've missed. There must be something here to dig at. Oh, and I'll have a look at that video myself," Tanya said.

Something, some sixth sense, sent a jolt of anticipation through her as the phone rang. The ones standing near to her heard her mutter. "Bugger." She glanced around as she picked up the handset. Those who knew her from past cases paused and watched her face.

"Right. There we are then. Baker. The guy who found our male body" – she paused – "dead in his car in the garage at his home. Pipe from the exhaust, doors and windows closed tight."

She should take Finch with her, of course she should. She looked around the room. "DS Harris, could you come with me, please?"

Before there was time for any comment, she grabbed her coat and strode out and along the corridor, Paul Harris rushing to catch up with her. "My car, I'll drop you back later."

Chapter 36

"So, what do we know?" Tanya glanced at Paul Harris who was reading the full report on his phone.

"Found by the gardener who heard the car running and broke into the garage. He dragged Baker out, but he was unresponsive. The paramedics weren't able to do anything, so that's where we're at right now. The first responder declared life extinct. Nobody else at the house. A car has been sent to fetch the wife from her office. The medical examiner and so on are on the way, they'll probably get there before we do."

The road outside Baker's house was lined with cars. The neighbours stood beside their gates in solemn groups. They must have known there would be little to see, but strobing blue lights and sirens had brought them out. The coroner's car was pulled into the driveway and officers were in the process of screening the area. Tanya and Paul had to pick their way through the equipment. They didn't go into the garage but stood near the door watching the activity.

She raised a hand to the medical examiner, not Simon this time but Lisa Cummings, a relative newcomer to the team at the morgue. She stood and crossed the garage from beside the big black Pajero. The windows at the side of the building had been opened and the ones in the front door had been smashed; glass littered the entrance.

Tanya shook hands with the doctor who had pulled off her gloves. "What do you think?" she asked.

"Well, all indications at the moment are that he asphyxiated on the fumes which entered the car by way of that pipe." She pointed across the garage. "The gardener broke in, tried to ventilate the area and what not, but it was already too late. I can't tell you any more until I finish my examination. As you see he was dragged onto the floor in the efforts to revive him, but it was no good."

"Note?"

"Nothing that I've seen." She indicated the team who were moving around quietly. "Your people haven't found one anywhere here, as far as I know. But there are more officers in the house."

"Okay. Thanks, Doctor. One of my team will attend the post-mortem if that's okay."

"Fine, probably tomorrow morning, I'll ask Moira to let you know."

In the house, Tanya searched out Dave Chance, the senior SOCO. "Quite the place this, eh?" he said. They gazed around at the artwork on the walls, the blonde wood floors, and antique furnishings. "Bit like my place actually."

Tanya grinned at him. "That right?"

"Yeah, I've got stairs and walls, floors, all of it." He smiled at her, acknowledging the daft back and forth. "Right, so, the only thing we've found of interest is an empty medicine packet in the kitchen; anxiolytics. The date on the packet is recent but the pills have all gone, and there's a glass on the counter – empty. We've bagged them."

"I know he was on medication for his nerves, so that sounds logical."

"Do you know him then?" Dave asked.

"No, not really. He's a witness, or rather he was – in my current case. One of them at any rate."

"Ah, I wondered why all the fuss, and then they said you were on the way."

"Did he leave a note?"

"We haven't found anything. They don't always, you know. If anything does show up, I'll give you a call. So, he's involved with the headless golfer?"

"He found the body – him and his friend," Tanya said.

"Bloody hell, not been a good week for him, has it?"

"No, I guess not. I'll leave you to it, Dave."

As she moved away, the car she had last seen outside the golf club, turned into the drive. The passenger door flew open and Patricia Baker stumbled out. As she went towards the open garage, one of the uniformed constables stepped in and turned her away. She didn't struggle but leaned to try and see past. They led her gently towards the house. A tall, dark-haired man climbed from the driver's side door and stood for a moment, unsure which direction to take; finally striding to the little group entering the front door and wrapping his arms around Tricia Baker's shoulders.

Chapter 37

"Perhaps we could sit in here?" As she spoke, Tanya indicated the room where they had interviewed Peter Baker on the visit just a few days previously. "I'm afraid there are people in the other rooms." She knew this space had already been screened and cleared.

"What exactly is going on?" This from the man who had driven the car.

"I'm sorry, who are you, sir?" Tanya asked.

"This is my brother, Robin – Robin Turner. But what is going on, what is all this…?" Tricia Baker's eyes flicked back and forth taking in the suited figures in her kitchen and hallway.

"I'm sorry, Mrs Baker; sir," Tanya said. "We're looking after your husband, and these other people are just trying to find out exactly what has happened."

"How long will it take?" There was a hint of hysteria as Tricia pushed to her feet and turned towards the door. Tanya strode across and laid a hand on her arm.

"I'm sorry, just at the moment that's not possible to say."

"They told me that I needed to come home, and now I find this – this pantomime." Tears had flooded her eyes and her brother handed her his handkerchief.

"As soon as possible I'll make sure you're given as much information as is available. Please try and be patient," Tanya said.

It seemed that it was suddenly too much, and the woman sank to the sofa and buried her face in her hands and sobbed. Robin Turner sat beside her and drew her into his arms. Raising his head, he addressed Tanya directly. "I don't think there is anything to be gained by you standing there. How long will all these people–" he waved a hand to encompass the rooms around them "– be here, and what exactly are they doing?"

"They are just making sure there is nothing that we should know about. You must be aware Mr Baker was involved in the discovery of a body in the last week, and we must be sure there's nothing to connect that crime to what has happened here today. It's just what we have to do. I'm sorry, I understand it's very upsetting. Maybe it would be better if you could go somewhere else?"

"No, no I want to be here," Tricia said.

Tanya did not want to become embroiled in a pointless conversation which could only cause more friction. She turned to pick up her bag. "I think your brother's right, Mrs Baker. For now, the best thing would be for me to leave you in peace and go and do my job. Do you need a doctor? Is there anyone else that I can contact for you?"

Robin Turner dragged himself away from his sister and stood. "We can manage, thank you. If we need anyone, we can contact them ourselves. Now, my sister could probably use some privacy and quiet."

As they made their way back towards the garage, Paul Harris sniffed. "Bit above himself under the circumstances, wasn't he? That Robin bloke."

"He's upset, I suppose, and a bit protective of his sister. There is one thing though that is a bit puzzling. Can you contact the officer who picked her up from her office, and find out exactly what she's been told?

"Apart from that, I don't think we can do anything else here so I'll drop you back, and we might as well call it a day, unless the rest of the team have anything more to tell us."

Chapter 38

The team was winding down by the time Tanya and Paul Harris arrived at the office. Jamie Mulholland was still missing, enquiries among his friends had led to nothing, and there was still no answer from his phone.

Tanya spent some time peering at the video, stopping and starting it, trying to zoom in to an image that was blurred and indistinct. "I can see what you mean," she told Kate. "But it's so unclear." She shook her head.

"Okay, tomorrow I'll have a word with the DCI, maybe we should get a warrant and search his place. It's odd that he's gone missing right now. We have to wait until tomorrow for confirmation about Peter Baker, but on the surface, it looks as though the horror simply became too much for him. But let's not jump to conclusions about that."

"How do you mean, boss?" Kate asked.

"Not sure, there was just something that seemed strange. I need to think about it. Mull it over. Let's keep an open mind. Where's DI Finch?"

"He left early, ma'am."

"Did he say why, Kate?"

The other woman looked uncomfortable and it was Sue Harris who spoke out. "He said he might just as well go and get an early night because there wasn't much for him to do."

Tanya caught the glimpse of something in the dark eyes of the younger officer. Devilment of some sort, a declaration of allegiance? He should have let her know that he was intending to slope off early, at least as a courtesy. He was the same rank now, but she was SIO; she would have to bring him back into line. Her heart sank at the thought of the confrontation. She really didn't need it.

* * *

Sitting in her living room later, a glass of wine on the table beside her laptop, she paused for thought. The house was quiet around her, the cleaner had been in again and there was a smell of polish and detergent. For the first time since Charlie had moved in all those weeks ago the house truly felt like her own space again. No Charlie, no Serena.

The silence was broken by the chime of her phone. She tutted but then, when she saw Charlie's ID, she smiled.

"Can you talk?" he asked.

"Yes, I'm at home. Just going over things, filling in my occurrence book. We had another death today. Looks like suicide but…"

"But?"

"Oh, I don't know, there's something in the back of my mind that just keeps niggling at me."

"Well, stick with it, Tanya. Your instincts have not let you down before. Remember that handbag?" He referred to a piece of evidence that had been a breakthrough and vital clue in Tanya's first major case. "Your gut has served you well in the past."

"Yeah. Anyway, what's happening?"

"I wanted to let you know about Jamie Mulholland. I've sent a copy of his records through, but I thought I'd give you a quick rundown. It's not much really."

"Oh, you found something then?"

"Yes, having his NI number made it easy. He was born in Kirkby, on the outskirts of 'The pool'."

He made her laugh by putting on a fake scouse accent.

"Parts of it, well most of it really, are pretty rough. He was what they call 'a bit of a scally.'"

"A scally – what's that?" Tanya asked.

She heard him chuckle.

"Well I suppose it must come from scallywag and that's about it really. In and out of trouble but nothing too serious. Him and his brother, Sean. Twocing, mostly older, cheap cars for a joy ride, the ones that are easy to get into and hot wire. A bit of shoplifting, the odd drunk and disorderly, just petty crime and nuisance really. Nothing for just over two years though."

"Oh, okay, that fits. I suppose he could have escalated, but why? I mean that all sounds like stuff that resulted from boredom and frustration, why murder? Unless he has got himself mixed up with a different group down here. Do we know where the brother is now?"

"Banged up for nine months. Due out in December – should be home with his mum for Christmas."

"Ha, nice."

"Yeah. A nice Irish family," he said. "There are aunties and uncles all over the place, cousins and what have you. Most of them are known to us. He didn't really stand much chance of keeping straight given his background."

"No, but still – murder, and chopping up corpses." She glanced at the screen, "I've got another call coming in, Charlie, can I call you back?"

"No, listen it's fine. I've sent you the files. I'll call later in the week, we can catch up – and Tanya…"

"Yes."

"Go with your gut."

She clicked to the incoming call; it was a number she didn't recognise but the voice was immediately familiar. "Tanya, it's Simon."

"Hello, Dr Hewitt, sorry – Simon. I didn't recognise your number."

"No, I'm using my personal phone. Listen I'd like a word with you. Could you meet me… in the morning perhaps?"

"Okay, will you come to the office."

"No, no. I'd rather speak away from the office. Could I see you at home, maybe in the morning? Is that okay?"

"Yep, I usually leave about seven thirty."

"Okay, I'll be there around seven. Goodnight, Tanya."

It was strange and puzzling but the next call just a half an hour later pushed Simon and his request from her mind. A sack torn open by foxes and rats and the scattered pieces of finger bones required all of her attention.

Chapter 39

It seemed like days that Ana had sat in silence. She wondered if her voice was gone forever and to find out, now and then she whispered her own name, low and careful. At first, she had been silent because she had been so afraid of what was going to happen to her. Nothing truly dreadful occurred, just the police's constant encouragement to tell them who she was, where she was from and who they could contact for her. But by now it was impossible to speak – there was no starting point anymore.

They had talked about court, about charges; she didn't really understand, so again she made no response. She wondered what had happened to the old woman. Maybe she was dead. If she was dead, then they might leave her here forever in this little room. Her mother would never know what had happened to her.

She needed to call her brother. It was the only thing she wanted to say, but to do that she would need to tell them where she was from. It would give them a way in, a way to get to the truth, or at least the parts of it that she could speak about.

Some of it was locked inside forever.

No matter what happened, she would never tell anyone about the drugs. Carried in her body and then expelled in the most degrading manner. Handed over to Bogdan, who had smirked at her as he held the little packages in his gloved fingertips. No, she would never speak of that. She would never speak about the nights that he had come, with his friends, and they turned the women into whores, with threats and violence and ugly sex. She would not speak of that, so she did not speak at all.

They wanted her to confide in them so they could call her embassy, or a solicitor, or her friends. These were the options they gave her; ways to make it all end.

Late in the afternoon, a policeman came to her. He had a woman with him – a solicitor. They asked if she would let this woman be her representative. She didn't answer because she had no way to tell if this was good or bad. They said she had broken the law but more than likely she would just be sent home. This must mean that the woman wasn't dead and she wasn't a killer. Tears had sprung to her eyes then and they had thought they were getting through and waited for her to break. She didn't and they brought her back to the tiny cell, the hard bed, the metal, unscreened toilet in the corner and the dry, tasteless food and beige drinks.

Thoughts swirled and circled in her brain. Now surely, it was far too late to call home. If the threats and promises were real, then her brother and mother might already be dead. They may be in pain, or even more terrified than she was, because they'd had no warning – pawns in a game that none of them knew they were playing. But, if they were empty words from the ugly mouth of Bogdan, then calling them now would cause panic and distress.

She could tell these people the truth. Tell them about the caravan, the work, the beatings and deprivation they were all suffering, and surely they would act.

This England didn't allow things like that, did it?

They would go and try to find out. Ah, but then, everyone would know who had told and for sure her mother would die, if not at the hands of Bogdan's friends, then in revenge by the other families. The others at the factory would be punished, and she couldn't let that happen. They had made their own decisions, had their own fears, and their own people in peril. No, she could not do that.

They had all signed contracts, they all owed him money and they had all brought drugs into the country. He said that he had proof, video of them swallowing the little packages at the house where they waited for the tickets, and then video of when they arrived in Dover. She believed that. She remembered the dark room, the man with the camera and Bogdan himself at the port clicking away with his phone. She should have refused, but by then she owed so much money. The bus trip through Europe, the ticket for the boat, and the money he said he'd paid to get her a job. She believed them when they said that everyone carried drugs and it would help to pay back the debt. She had believed him because there was no option.

Perhaps she was wrong. Could it be that the right thing to do now was to ask for help, tell the truth, the truths that she could speak at least? What was the worst that could happen? They would send her home, but they were going to do that anyway, and by now it was all she wanted. She wanted to go home. She wanted to feel her mother's arms around her, and she wanted to sit on the steps of their little house with her brother and drink beer until the stars began to spin and the world began to tip, and he laughed at her and helped her to bed.

Because she didn't know which of her tumbled thoughts to tell them, she told them nothing. They gave up and said she must wait now for people to come from the immigration department, then they would decide what to do with her. So, she waited for many hours punctuated only by the screams of drunks and the clink and clang of metal and the dull thud of boots.

The door of the little cell opened and the young policewoman who had found her in the alley stepped inside. She had a white plastic bag in her hand. "Hello. I'm sorry you're still here. I just spoke to the sergeant. The immigration officers can't make it until tomorrow now. I thought you might like this. We're not supposed to do this, but…." She shrugged and smiled. "I didn't know what you liked. This is from the Polish restaurant, I thought maybe, you know, you would like it better than ham sandwiches and shepherd's pie."

She pulled the plastic boxes from the bag and a smell almost like home filled the small, mean space and Ana began to cry.

Chapter 40

Simon wasn't there. Tanya hadn't really expected him to be. This wasn't a body, but a collection of bones, spread and gnawed at by the rats and foxes. If the little terrier, sitting quietly now at the feet of his shocked and shaken owner, hadn't found the remains instead of the rabbit he was supposed to be rooting out, then the evidence would have been lost, most probably forever.

A forensic team was on their knees, floodlit in the damp undergrowth. Small yellow evidence tents had been placed where bones lay around the piece of torn sacking. Photographers recorded the activity and there was the quiet hum of subdued voices. It was understated and calm – so unlike the first discovery. Because of the spread of bones, they hadn't erected a tent over the scene: it was so far away from the road that there wasn't much chance of the public turning up, and it was too late to protect what evidence there was from the weather.

They should be able to avoid the press and the ghouls, for the time being at least. That was of course unless the dog owner had used his phone and was itching to get off somewhere so he could enjoy his moment of fame on the internet.

Tanya interviewed him and asked him to exercise discretion lest he frustrate her enquiries, but that was all she could do.

Although she had suited up, Tanya didn't push all the way forward through the damp grass; there was no point. If these were the remains of the man in the hut, then she would be told soon enough. If they weren't then she didn't need to get in the way of the experts.

She turned to Paul Harris. "Right, well, I don't reckon we are going to achieve much hanging around here. I'm sorry, I guess there was no need to call you out."

"It's okay, ma'am, the wife's got friends round. It's all chardonnay and sobbing at my place. I might go into work anyway and go through some reports on the phone calls."

Tanya was impressed; at last, it seemed that he was getting himself together. "Great. That'll be helpful."

"Yeah, well, like DI Finch says, you have to put in the miles to get anywhere."

"Oh, he says that, does he?"

"Yes, and he should know. He's one of the youngest DIs in the county. Well, I mean, I know you were when you first got your promotion but, you know seeing him, seeing how he's got on." He shrugged. "It just made me realise I've been lagging behind a bit. You know it's easier for a woman, all this positive bias there is these days. Quotas for females in higher office, all that malarkey. It has to ease the way for you, doesn't it? We've still got to do it the hard way, us blokes."

Tanya turned away so that he wouldn't see how much he'd angered her. She clenched her teeth. She had encouraged him, as much as she could, given his previous laziness and careless attitude. She knew that Charlie had as well. So, it took Brian Finch with his money and his connections, his flash car and big desk, to give Paul the push that he'd needed. As for the rest of it – his misogynistic comments – she was furious. People like Paul would never understand; it was almost not their fault because they had a huge blind spot as far as sexual equality was concerned, but that didn't help. Right then in the dark woods she really wanted nothing more than to slap him across his face. That would be the end of her career. It would be a win for people like him who, even now, after all the struggle, didn't take women seriously.

She took a breath, spoke as calmly as she could. "I'm going to assume this is our victim. We're only a couple of miles from the golf course, and surely the whole of this area isn't just a body dump." She pulled a face at him. "Hmm, even that's possible, I suppose; who can tell these days? But from what I've been told by the woman over there…" She pointed. "I can't remember her name now. Find out will you, we might need to speak to her later. Anyway, what she said was that there was still flesh on the bones. Some of the phalanges." She raised her brows at his expression. "That's fingers to you and me, Paul. Well some of them were still connected with tissue."

"Right, so they aren't ancient?"

"Apparently not. There's no skull though. Just small bones of the hands and wrists, some of the radius. That's one of the arm bones here." She pointed at her lower arm on the side nearest to her thumb. "The forensic woman says that, from what she's been able to see here, it has been cut through fairly cleanly. But, of course, she's hampered by the location and what not right now. She's going to get back to me as soon as she has anything and reckons that it won't be long before they can at least confirm if this is the rest of our golf course man. Did you know they were calling him, 'the headless golfer'?"

Harris shook his head. "I didn't. Always got to go with buzz words and titles, don't they?"

"Yes, it seems like it. Nothing we can do about that."

"I guess not, boss."

She noted his use of the address, a courtesy and not much more than habit. It actually made her rather sad given his previous comments. She pushed the thoughts aside. "No. But there we are, it's a bit of drama for the masses I suppose, sells better than 'dead ordinary bloke'."

She turned away, pulling at the paper suit. "I'll be in about seven-thirty in the morning. See you then."

"Oh, boss. Just before you go," Harris said. "I eventually traced the uniform car that went to Tricia Baker's workplace. The people at the scene had no bloody idea who'd been sent for her. Well, she drove herself home, didn't she? At least that snotty brother did. Anyway, I had to go back to dispatch. Eventually spoke to the female officer myself."

"Right – and?"

In response, the sergeant shook his head. "They didn't have much information, were simply sent to tell her there had been an emergency, that her husband was involved, and she should go home. She refused the offer of a lift and the brother took over from there. That was it. Job done, they just went back on patrol."

"Where is it she works again?"

He took out his notebook and peered at it. "Woodbarn something or other."

"I thought it was a farm?"

"I think it was, a long time ago, but now it's just poultry. Chickens mostly. Turkeys at Christmas, that sort of thing." He was looking up the details on his phone. "It's apparently medium sized in the industry. Still a family concern though."

"Hmm. Did you ask what her reaction was when they went to collect her?" Tanya said.

"I did, but the WPC wasn't very helpful, hadn't registered much. Just said Mrs Baker called her brother – he works at the same place, so he was nearby. Then she thanked them, and they left. What are you looking for?"

Tanya shook her head. "Not sure yet, just something that's niggling me. Leave it with me for now."

"Boss. Right, if that's it, I'll see you in the morning."

Chapter 41

The text from Simon Hewitt pinged as Tanya climbed back into her bed. It was a brief apology. He'd been called out to a body and didn't think that he could make it for breakfast. Tanya double checked her calls and texts but there was nothing for her, so she responded with a suggestion that they meet for lunch if he was free, turned out the light and was asleep within minutes.

Kate Lewis was in the office first the next morning. She had already started another board with images of the scattered bones and the torn sacking. She had drawn an arrow towards the images of the first dreadful discovery in the hut at the golf course, but it ended with a large question mark. Tanya nodded her approval. "Chase them will you, Kate. The woman I spoke to last night said it wouldn't take them long. We need to know as quickly as possible if this is our first victim, well, little teeny bits of him at any rate."

"Yes, boss, there's a search going on for the rest of the bones and the skull; they called a halt last night when it started to rain again. They should be back there now."

"Excellent. Anything else?"

"You had a call on the internal phone, from the DCI's office. He'd like a word, soon as you can."

"Okay. Is DI Finch in the office yet?"

"Not yet, ma'am."

Tanya glanced around; the rest of them had arrived. They booted up their devices, stuffed coats and bags into drawers, and sipped at take away coffees. They were ready for another day of slogging through routines, waiting for the bright flash of a breakthrough.

It didn't set the right example. DI or not, he should be here if the team were, unless he was in the field, but she didn't see how that could be. She'd deliberately been cutting him out. She really must stop it. What was it about him that made her wary of treating him as an equal, or at least as one of the team? She didn't know. Maybe it was just that she wanted him to be Charlie. Well, he wasn't, and they had to get through it. She'd have to speak to him for her own sake as well as his. Her stomach twisted at the thought of it.

In the office, the drinks machine was turned on and there was a small white cup on the table, dregs in the bottom. She picked up the cup and tilted it. The tiny puddle of coffee ran back and forth. Not yesterday's then, that would have been a dried smudge by now. She went behind the new desk. His laptop bag was on the floor beside the chair and his computer was turned on. Her fingers itched to slide the mouse across the desk, just one little nudge would do it – at least she would be able to see if he'd been looking at something. Chances were, of course, there would just be the force logo swimming across a blue background. That was the way it should be. She stretched out a finger. Footsteps echoed in the corridor outside and she flew like a guilty child back to her own desk, threw herself into the chair and began to boot up her own machine.

Kate stepped into the office. "Ma'am, I've been on to the morgue. That Moira was on duty." She pulled a face. It was never easy dealing with the dragon woman who ran the reception for the medical examiners as if it was her own fiefdom. "There's a report coming through. All she was authorised to tell me was that, from their preliminary examination, they would say that the bones found in the wood are a match for the body in the hut. The cuts on the end of the radius match. They have taken DNA of course, but it'll be a bit before we have results."

"Was there any chance of fingerprints, from the skin and flesh that was left?"

"No, boss. I did ask."

"Hmm, that's what I thought. They were pretty damaged but there was apparently some flesh, it was just an outside chance. Right, I'm off to see DCI Scunthorpe. We'll have a briefing when I get back. I wish we could find the skull. Maybe there would be enough to put together an image. Nothing back from the posters of the young woman?"

"Nothing yet, boss. I think the people in the press department are going to try and get it on the next Crimewatch programme – that's next week."

"Brilliant. I didn't know about that though, it's not in my messages."

"No, ma'am." Kate reddened. "I think it was DI Finch who was liaising. I think he was going to do the interview."

"Where did you hear that?"

"A mate in the press office. Actually, he rang to ask if you'd been taken off the case because he thought it was a bit odd."

Tanya was embarrassed. It wasn't that she wanted to go on the television, she hated the idea and had managed to avoid it up until now. But as SIO, she should be the one, if anyone from the investigation was to do it. Maybe her interview with Bob Scunthorpe would shed some light on what exactly was going on. A worm of fear curled in the back of her brain. She hadn't made much progress. Nothing at all in truth, and there were more bodies. Had

she screwed up so much that she was going to be replaced
by Brian Finch?

Chapter 42

Bob had a new secretary. When had that happened? And where was the pleasant young woman who always seemed to be on Tanya's side?

"Go right in, Detective Inspector."

Tanya knocked once on the door, stepped in and there was Brian Finch, deep in conversation with the DCI.

"Tanya, good morning. Coffee?" Bob stood and walked around his desk, shook her hand, indicated a chair opposite where Finch sat, looking very relaxed.

"No, no coffee, thanks, sir." Though she refused the drink, Tanya had no choice but to sit. She usually tried to keep these meetings short, standing just a step inside the door. It was necessary to keep the DCI informed and up to date, but she much preferred to do it by phone or email. He was a good boss, fair and supportive, but she would much rather work on a case than talk about it. Brian Finch raised his eyebrows as she moved the chair an infinitesimal distance away from him, turning it slightly so that she was facing more towards Bob Scunthorpe than him. She knew it was petty, but he made her feel awkward and she had the feeling, growing daily, that he wasn't to be trusted.

"Tanya." Scunthorpe leaned towards her, his forearms resting on the table, his fingers twined together. "We need to have a talk about your new assistant. We are going to have to have a change of direction." He glanced at Brian Finch who beamed back at him.

Tanya's heart jumped. Had he complained? Had the side-lining been too obvious? She had been warned that he had connections.

She clasped her fingers together, laid her hands on her lap and summoned up a smile.

"Right, sir." She nodded.

The DCI shuffled some of the papers in the file on his desk. "I don't imagine you've had a chance to go through the overnight reports yet?"

Tanya shook her head.

"Well, we had another suspicious death yesterday. A young woman, beaten and abandoned in Wolvercote Cemetery."

Tanya pulled out her phone. "I had nothing, sir."

"No, you wouldn't. It doesn't on the face of it look as though it's connected with your own enquiry. This victim was certainly killed unlawfully, but the body was in one piece, head, hands, the lot. So, it's a new enquiry. We're going to be stretched pretty thinly. Accordingly, I have asked DI Finch here to concentrate on this newest discovery. We'll have to split your team, for the time being at least. As you're already set up in your shared office, that should work. Well, there'll be a separate incident room, of course, and we've already generated a name for this enquiry."

"Yes sir, 'Blackbird'," Finch said.

Scunthorpe nodded and made a note on his pad. "I'll leave the fine details regarding manpower deployment to be sorted between yourselves. For the time being at least, you are going to lose your wing man I'm afraid." He smiled at Tanya, sympathetically.

Yes!

Tanya kept her face neutral and made a couple of affirmative grunts. She glanced across at Finch to see the hint of a smirk on his face. Could it be that he was pleased to be given his own major case so soon? Could it be that he could see right into her head, could detect the overwhelming sense of relief?

DCI Scunthorpe pushed back his chair, the meeting at an end.

Tanya raised a hand. "There is just one thing, sir? Detective Lewis mentioned that we are hoping for a spot on Crimewatch, with the picture of our female victim?" She glanced at Brian Finch. "I believe it was the plan that, Detective Inspector Finch would do the interview?"

"I haven't read my memos from the press office this morning." As he spoke the DCI moved the mouse on his desk and began to scroll.

"I just wondered if this new situation would change that plan, sir?" Tanya waited as he leaned forward, obviously reading his screen.

"Yes, I see this now. Hmm. That was the plan yes. Apparently, the television people prefer a male officer." He glanced across the desk. "Sorry, Tanya. That's not acceptable, I'll have a word."

She could tell that he was uncomfortable and was sorry now that she had spoken. She liked her boss, and this wasn't his doing.

"I don't mind, sir, I didn't really want to do it, I just thought that, as Detective Inspector Finch is going to be working on his own case…"

"Yes, quite," Bob Scunthorpe muttered.

Brian Finch said, "It's just that they find the public respond better to a male officer in uniform. I know someone down in the press office, he explained it to me. It's all a bit non-PC but… well, whatever gets the job done, I suppose."

Bob Scunthorpe turned away from his screen. "Leave this with me, would you? I need to have a word with a couple of people. But as it's already been arranged, are you happy for DI Finch to do the interview?"

"Yes, sir. No problem."

There was no other answer that she could give, but Tanya caught the flash of smugness on Brian Finch's face, that was definitely one score to him. "Unless we have a major breakthrough, of course," she said.

At least she had the last word.

Chapter 43

They left the DCI's office and walked side by side along the corridor. "I'll take Kate and Paul, if that's okay," Brian Finch said.

Tanya bit back her explosive response. Okay, this was a declaration of war. He knew, he just had to know, they were the people she needed the most, and he knew why.

She drew in a breath and shook her head. "Well, that won't work for me, I'm afraid. As you know Kate is my most computer savvy officer. You've done courses from what I've heard and there are the civilians, most of them are very skilled." She glanced at his profile, saw the jump of a nerve in his jaw. "And Paul, Detective Sergeant Harris, has been working very closely with me on my case. I've been impressed by his improved attitude and I reckon to move him now might give the wrong impression. No, I think it would be better if you took Detectives Price and Rollinson. I can cover their work with civilians."

She knew it would be hard for him to argue. Though she didn't have seniority of rank, she did have more time served in her present position and the arguments were fair and valid.

He didn't speak again, but he lengthened his stride and stomped ahead of her. As they reached the incident room he leaned around the door. "Detective Price, Detective Rollinson, could I have a word?"

It was wrong, completely out of order, but she could hardly have a verbal battle with him in front of the team. She turned into their shared office and, yes, it was the devil on her shoulder that made her do it, but she walked over to the machine and began to make herself a cappuccino.

It was a stressful, awkward morning; there was much muttering. The only one completely happy with the new arrangement was Sue Rollinson, who threw herself into helping set up the new incident room. They reassigned some of the civilians who simply went where they were told, the politics much less important to them, though she imagined they had their own conflicts. Wherever there were people, you had battles for supremacy. It was one of the reasons she admired Kate Lewis. The woman truly just wanted to get the job done and the rest of it didn't bother her.

* * *

By lunch time Tanya had the start of a headache and her shoulders were aching with tension. She met Simon Hewitt at a coffee shop near to the morgue.

"You alright, Tanya?" he asked.

"Yes, thanks. It's been a bit of a morning to be honest and I can do without it right now. I need to move things along with this golf club case. I'm trying to find the bar manager. I've asked for a warrant to search his place and had to jump through some hoops for it because we are so short on information. He might be completely uninvolved, but it's odd that he's disappeared right now. On top of that, there's something niggling at me about the suicide, but I don't want to speak too soon or cause trouble unnecessarily and send us all off on a wild goose chase. I need more on that. Then to top it all, I've lost half my team to another case."

He nodded quietly. "Is that the body from last night?"

"Yes, DI Finch has been assigned, but we're short of officers, well, you know that. Oh well, I'll just have to get on with it. I can't deal with the politics though, I never have been able to, and right now it feels as though personalities are gumming up the works."

She stopped herself, this wasn't her, she didn't share her failings. Growing up in the shadow of her older sister she had felt failure and weakness more deeply than someone from a more balanced family might have done. To hear herself admit now that there were things she found it hard to deal with took her by surprise. She looked up at Simon Hewitt. He was watching her with concern.

"I'm going to do the post-mortem exam on the poor woman this afternoon. On the face of it, it seems that she's been beaten to death. I suppose this means that DI Finch will be attending?"

"I imagine so. He's got Dan and Sue with him."

"Ah, I like Dan, he's got what it takes, I reckon." The fact that he didn't mention Sue Rollinson spoke volumes and Tanya smiled across the table.

"Was there any special reason why you wanted to meet, Simon? I mean it's lovely and all, it really is, especially after the morning I've had." She paused as their lunches were delivered and there was the fuss of utensils, and water, and tomato sauce for Simon's chips.

When it was all done, Simon took up the conversation. "From what you've said I think maybe the main reason I wanted to have a chat has already been negated. To lay my cards on the table, I've been a little concerned about Brian Finch's behaviour."

Tanya tipped her head to one side, sipped at her glass of water and waited.

"I don't know if you were aware, but he's been visiting the morgue quite regularly, asking questions. Of course, he doesn't often get past Moira." He laughed. "Still, she mentioned it to me. She felt at first that he was simply being over-enthusiastic, his first big case as a DI and so on and of course it could just be that. I was bothered by the feeling that he was working on his own more than I would have expected. Turning up after hours and speaking to the assistants, a couple of them had noticed it. He had asked to see the body again."

"But what was he asking about? I mean we've all seen your reports – he has full access to all of that."

"Yes, indeed. But he has visited every day, wondering if we have had DNA results, wondering if we are any nearer to finding out the nationality of our victim. All perfectly reasonable but, well... I don't think I've had so much intense follow up of a case before and I just thought you should know about it. I didn't imagine you were behind it. I was leaning towards the idea that he wanted to be the first to know about everything. Wanted to be the one to shine. It's not useful is it, having people pursuing their own agendas? Mind you, if he has been assigned a case of his own now, that should keep him busy."

"Yes, but you're the medical examiner on that one. If this is the way that he's going to work, it's going to be a bit of a pain for you," Tanya said.

"Ha, not really. If I tell Moira to keep him back, well..." He shrugged. "To be honest though, I've rather wanted to see you outside of work for a while, Tanya." His voice had dropped as he looked down at the table, fiddled with his fork. "I guess this is hardly outside of work, seeing as that's all we've talked about. But I just wondered if maybe you'd like to have dinner with me some time?"

Tanya glanced around the restaurant. Did she want to do this? Did she want to become involved personally with anyone, and especially someone with whom she worked? It had been a long time since she'd been in a relationship and that hadn't ended well. Police work often made private life difficult and complicated. Unless someone was in the job it was hard for them to understand. Apart from that, she preferred her own space, her own company and the freedom to concentrate totally on the job; her career. But it had been such a difficult morning; she felt tired and despondent. He was only asking her to have dinner with him, and he was aware, as much as anyone could be, of the demands of the work. She put down her knife and fork and looked across at him.

Chapter 44

Back at work, Tanya brought DS Paul Harris into the office and they went over the interview, such as it had been, with Tricia Baker. She asked him again about the car sent to collect her from work. She didn't tell him what was bothering her. If he had independently voiced concerns that matched her own, then it would have given her more confidence. As it was, she decided to sit on it for the time being.

"I think we'll go and have another word with Mrs Baker, maybe after she's had a chance to see her husband's body. Keep an eye on that for me, let me know when it's done. Oh, hang on, wasn't Sue Rollinson going to attend. Find out when it's scheduled, I'll go myself," she said.

Kate Lewis interrupted their meeting with the news that the warrant had come through for them to search Jamie Mulholland's flat.

"What are we looking for, boss?" Harris asked as they walked to the car.

"To be honest with you, Paul, I can't really say. It's a bit odd, him vanishing right now. I've been in touch with Charlie up in Liverpool and it seems that Mulholland has a bit of a spotty past. It feels like clutching at straws, I know, but I reckon it's worth us having a look at least. There is that video of the white van. It could be him," Tanya said.

"How's DI Lambert?"

"Yes, he's okay. Seems to have settled down well anyway, and his wife's doing better."

"So, if this search doesn't throw up anything, what then?" Harris asked.

Now would be the time to share her thoughts with regard to Tricia Baker, but as it was unformed and insubstantial, she held her peace. "We go back and look at everything again. We cross our fingers that someone recognises our female victim, and we keep working at it."

"Seems like DI Finch has got an easier case. I mean some woman battered in a graveyard. That's got to be more straightforward, hasn't it? Probably some street walker upset a client, or a domestic. Yeah, bet it'll turn out to be a domestic. Nice quick clear up for him. Nice brownie points."

"Would you rather have been with him then, Paul?"

For a moment he didn't speak, when he did it was quietly, thoughtfully. "No, no. I reckon that brownie points are all well and good, especially if I'm going to put in for promotion, but this is harder, isn't it? More challenging."

It looked as though maybe she hadn't misjudged the change in his attitude. "You seem more focused lately, Paul, is that all down to him – to Finch?"

"I've got to say he made me think. The wife's on at me anyway, wants to move out of the flat, get a house – nagging and whinging. I thought, well, if I get my promotion, it might keep her quiet for a while, give her something to brag to her sisters about."

She didn't know if that were true or whether it was swagger. He was still a bit of a prat, just a more ambitious prat seemingly.

"I hear he's been visiting the morgue a lot, DI Finch. Following up every day. Do you know anything about that?"

"No. Can I speak freely, boss?"

"Of course, Paul."

"I liked him, when he came in. I was impressed, I won't lie. His flash car, the suit. I asked around about him – he's a highflyer, isn't he?"

Tanya didn't answer, she waited for him to continue.

"He's a laugh, I'll give him that." He paused for a moment. "I think we're better this way though, boss. I was a bit bothered about the questions he was asking, some of the stuff he wanted to know. Yeah, I reckon this has been a good thing. We can manage with the smaller team and it'll be good experience for Dan. Sue's in her element as well, fluttering her eyelashes at him."

Tanya let the comment about Sue Rollinson go. "What sort of questions?"

"Well about you, boss. I mean most people know about your first case, how you were nearly killed, and then about that incident in Scotland when you were hurt. Well, we know you've got balls, ma'am."

Tanya splurted out a laugh and he joined in from the passenger seat.

"Sorry, that was out of order I suppose. But I mean it. Finch though, he wanted to know other stuff, who you lived with, about you and Charlie."

"What?"

"Yeah. I mean we all know that Charlie is besotted with Carol and totally nuts about his little boy. Charlie would never do anything to risk that."

She noted that her morals weren't part of his thinking.

"We know why he was staying at your place. I didn't like what he was inferring, and I would have told him so, if it'd come to it. DI or not."

Hmm, he'd just gone down a bit on the prattish scale.

"Well, thanks for that, Paul, I appreciate it. If he wants to know any more about my private life, just refer him to me, will you?"

She pulled into the kerbside now and pointed to a small blue van parked in front of them. "Ha, the locksmith's here. Let's go and see if Mr Mulholland was hiding anything of interest."

Chapter 45

Though it had never been said aloud, Tanya was alert to the possibility of the smell of decay and death in the small flat. There had been so much death in such a short space of time that, if they had found Jamie Mulholland slumped in his chair, or worse, she would not have been surprised.

In the event, the flat smelled faintly of old cooking and dust. It was reasonably tidy: the kitchen surfaces were clear, and the Formica tops wiped clean. A couple of mugs sat on the draining board, one washed out the other with dried dregs in the bottom. The place felt abandoned, but only in the way of a house where the occupants were away for a long holiday.

Paul Harris ran his finger over the desk in the corner. "No computer? I've looked in the bedrooms, both of them. There's the electrical extension underneath and marks on the top, there's the printer, but no actual computer."

"I suppose he could just have a laptop and have it with him; mind you, I don't think you do that if you've just popped out for a bit. Or maybe you do. Have you looked in the wardrobes?" Tanya asked.

"No, not yet. I've just done a quick scan of the rooms, just in case, you know?"

So, he'd thought the same as she had – that they might find another corpse.

"I'll do the main bedroom now." Paul turned and went back down the little hallway. She heard the click of cupboard doors and the rattle of coat hangers.

It was bland and bare, like a holiday let waiting for tenants. Cups and plates in cupboards. A few opened packets of pasta, rice, biscuits but no food in the fridge which smelled stale because it had been switched off with the door closed.

Paul re-joined her. "He's done a runner, hasn't he? There's just a couple of pairs of jeans, old and worn, no underwear. No socks. There's a couple of towels in the airing cupboard and that's it. There's soap in the bathroom but the sink is dry."

"You didn't run water, did you?"

Paul glared at her as Tanya blurted out the question, and she knew what a mistake she'd made. "Sorry. Of course you didn't. Sorry."

He inclined his head in acknowledgement but still turned away with a huff of anger. "I'll organise a team, shall I? Forensics?"

"I think so. We'd better just secure the place and leave it to them. There's nothing to indicate that he cut up a body in this place, is there? Surely you couldn't do that and leave no trace. I don't see anything to suggest that sort of mayhem. It's just empty."

"No, but if there is anything to find, we'll find it."

"Yep. But you know, I just feel as though there's nothing here. I don't think there has been murder and dismemberment done in this place. I know it's unscientific but…" She left the sentence unfinished. She couldn't adequately explain it, because it was the absence of evil and that sounded far too wacky to share with down-to-earth

Sergeant Harris. Anyway, her phone was vibrating in her pocket.

She held up the small device. "Text from Detective Lewis. Tricia Baker is going to see her husband's body. I want to be there. Can I leave you to sort stuff out here? I'll send a car to take you back."

"Yes, that's fine. Oh, and boss…"

She waited.

"I'll be sure not to take a piss."

She couldn't be offended because as he spoke his eyes sparkled with mischief and she knew that, really, she deserved the put down for having so little confidence in him.

"Right," she said. "See that you don't."

Chapter 46

Tanya called Kate Lewis as soon as she was in her car on the way to the morgue. "We need CCTV from around the area of Jamie Mulholland's flat. Have some of the civilians viewing it as soon as possible. Get in touch with DI Lambert up in Liverpool. I'll ping you his number. Ask him to expedite the report, we need a picture of Mulholland. They must have one because he's known to them. We need to find him. It's possibly far too late, but can you call the DCI and ask him to clear an All Ports Alert. Can I leave all this with you for now, Kate? I need to meet up with Mrs Baker for the viewing of her husband."

"It's okay, ma'am. I'm on it."

Kate, one of the most efficient and effective officers she'd worked with, was still a detective constable – it was wrong. When all this work was out of the way she would have another try. Encourage her to have a go at promotion to sergeant. She deserved it and it would be a good thing for the force. She was being wasted.

The big four-wheel drive that belonged to Tricia Baker's brother was already in the car park when Tanya arrived. They were waiting in a small family room. The woman was nervous and pale; her brother paced back and forth across the meagre space, glancing at his watch regularly. Everyone dealt with horror in a different way and it wasn't any sort of indication of their true feelings. She had known relatives break down to the extent that they needed to be almost carried out of the viewing room. Others were stoic verging on cold, but often they were the ones who were most deeply affected and were simply able to hold themselves together better.

Tricia Baker hit about the middle of the reactions scale. She nodded briefly to confirm that the body was her husband. There was no doubt, but i's had to be dotted and t's crossed. Tears trickled across her cheek and she dabbed at them with a tissue. Robin Turner put his arms around her shoulders and led her back into the corridor. Tanya thanked the technician and then hurried after them.

"Can I get you anything, Mrs Baker?" She caught up with them almost at the door.

"No, thank you. I just want to go home now."

Tanya moved around so that she was between the couple and the exit. She held out her hand which Tricia Baker shook briefly, frowning at her and then attempting to move past. "If there is anything you need at all, you have my number," Tanya said.

"Yes, thank you." She was still pushing forward.

"I trust my team have been looking after you?" This was a twist of truth – it hadn't been her team, but she assumed Tricia would have no idea of the organisation of the enquiries. "It's obviously been a dreadful shock."

"Yes, yes." Robin Turner held up a hand, trying to clear the way.

"I trust they were sensitive? When they brought you the news? It's a difficult part of the job, especially when relatives are away from home. As you were – in your office."

"They were fine. It was fine."

"Terrible for you, hearing that your husband was dead, under those circumstances."

"Yes, it was. But they were fine, well as good as they could be, you know. It was a shock. They offered me a lift home, but Robin was there, he took me. Well, you know that. You were there. Now, if you don't mind, I just want to get away from here."

"Sorry, sorry, yes of course. Please don't hesitate to call me if there is anything I can do."

She watched them cross the car park and clamber into their car. It was still insubstantial. She hadn't got the confirmation that she needed but for now, she would have to just let it be.

Chapter 47

Still nothing solid to work with and the case was growing colder. It had been five days since the discovery of the first body and they were no nearer to even identifying him. They had not found the skull. It was a mire of meagre information, supposition, and confusion.

Tanya flung her bag on the floor, slumped into her chair and lay her head on the desk. DI Finch must have heard her coming into their office and she raised her head as he coughed quietly from the doorway.

"You okay, Tanya?" he said.

"Fine, just tired you know. I've been missing a bit of sleep. How are you getting on with your body?" She would be polite, she would be professional, and she would make sure that, as far as possible, she would never work with him again.

"Yeah, early days. Just getting things organised, you know. I've got house to house organised for around the cemetery. We are waiting for Hewitt to get on with the post-mortem. Can't do much more until we have a specific cause of death."

It wasn't true, there was a lot he could do; she saw it for what it was, covering up the fact that he was stuck as much as she was. Still, it was very early days. Unless the scene was a kitchen with the murderer standing over the body, holding a knife dripping in blood, there was always a period of time collecting the facts, listing the suspects. Steps that had to be followed to make sure that if and when a case was presented to the CPS, it was water tight. It was tempting to rush headlong but that could end in disaster. There was a time when gung-ho detectives forged forward regardless and those cases had often come unravelled, sometimes even years later.

She pushed back her chair and went out into her own incident room. Kate Lewis stood when she saw her. "Boss, I didn't know you were back —I was just sending you a message."

Tanya could tell from the beaming smile that she had news. "Right – tell me something good, Kate."

"I reckon you'll like this. Tony…" She waved towards one of the civilians who was glued to his computer screen. He glanced up and raised his hand. "Tony spotted Mulholland on the CCTV, driving the white van three days ago. Leaving the parking area near his flat. He got us a registration number. We've tracked him using ANPR and the last sighting was today at Dover."

"Shit, does that mean we've just missed him?" Tanya said, kicking out at the nearest desk.

"Ha!" Kate laughed. "No, this is the good bit. He was spotted entering the country. He was coming back. I was just about to contact you. We're still tracking him. Do you want him stopped?"

The tiredness dissipated, Tanya could feel her nerves begin to spark, her brain buzzing. "No, not right away. Where is he now," she asked.

"On the M25 at the moment, just past Clacket Lane services. We've got a traffic officer in a car watching him and the cameras are recording his progress," Kate said.

"M25, Clacket Lane. So, chances are he's heading back this way. Let's just watch him."

It was exciting, a positive move, and yet in the back of her mind was the disturbing little suspicion that, if he was heading home from a trip to France, then he had nothing to hide, and they were wasting their time. She had no choice but to have him watched, but Tanya had a horrible feeling that what in the first moments had felt like a breakthrough, could quite easily be a total flop.

"What about the dodgy rear light?" she asked.

Tony shook his head. "No way to tell, all this is daytime."

"He could have fixed it anyway. Going to France, they'll pull you over for that," Kate said.

Chapter 48

Karen Laidlaw was about to finish her shift when the call came to let her know immigration officers were finally on their way to collect Ana.

"I know you're off duty in half an hour, but I thought you might like to know anyway," the sergeant told her.

"I'll come in if that's okay? I'd like to say goodbye and let her see a friendly face."

"Okay, in you come then. We're putting her in one of the interview rooms, ask at the desk when you arrive."

By the time Karen reached the station, Ana was sitting in one of the nicer interview rooms, one of the 'soft' spaces. The table and chairs there weren't screwed to the floor. Though it was bare and sparse it didn't have the threatening feel of the places used to intimidate suspects, to let them know they were not there for fun. There was a cup of tea cooling on the table and the girl's eyes, wide and frightened, were wet with tears. There was a female police officer sitting beside her, texting on her phone.

The tense set of her shoulders relaxed just a little, and there was an easing of the lines of fear on her forehead as Ana saw a familiar face. "Hello. I just thought I'd pop in and say goodbye," Karen said.

She still didn't speak, but for the first time since her nightmare had started, Ana managed a smile.

"Do you know what's going to happen? They are taking you to a holding centre until a decision is made about what to do. You can help yourself, you know. If you prove that you have a right to be in the country then, all this will go away. We are not going to do anything about the phone and the old lady. We know that you probably didn't mean to hurt her."

Ana would have grasped at the straw that was offered, but she knew that to prove who she was, she would have to tell them how she came into the country. She would have to explain why she didn't have her passport, tell them where she had been. It was impossible. It would hurt too many other people and there was still the chance they would find out about the smuggled drugs. It was possible that Bogdan would give them all up. If he thought it would help to save himself, he wouldn't hesitate.

She shook her head.

The door opened to two immigration officers. The small space was crowded now with uniforms and Karen could see that the girl was beginning to panic. She reached out and touched her arm. "It's alright. Nobody is going to hurt you."

The girl grabbed at her hand, squeezing it tightly in her terror. Karen eased the fingers gently with her other hand but still allowing Ana to hold on. They didn't handcuff her but positioned themselves one on either side. At the doorway there was a shuffle with not enough room for them all to pass through together, and Ana wasn't letting go of Karen's hand. In the end, the immigration team split, one in front and one behind, and in this strange procession, they made their way along the corridors towards the rear entrance.

"I have to go now. I'll try and keep in touch. If I can. Good luck." Karen could feel tears gathering in the back of her throat. She wondered, not for the first time, whether she was really cut out for the job.

Outside, in the gathering dusk, Ana's eyes flicked back and forth. It was starting to rain, the clouds of drizzle lit by lamps in the car park. She looked at the van pulled up to the rear doors of the building and then back along the corridor where they had just walked. It seemed she might run, but there was nowhere to run to. She stopped, raised her hand, her eyes wide and shocked.

The immigration woman grabbed out at her. "Come on love, don't let's have any trouble. It won't help."

As they shuffled her out of the narrow doorway, Ana twisted backwards, "Please, is Dani. Is my friend. Please tell her where I am."

It made no sense until, as they hustled her into the back of the van, Karen realised just what had attracted Ana's attention. On the noticeboard by the door, the image, with the usual 'Do You Know This Woman?' banner underneath.

She ran from the building waving her arms in a vain attempt to attract the attention of the van driver. "Wait, wait. Stop." It was no good, they were gone.

Karen grabbed the poster and ran back down the corridor to the front desk.

Chapter 49

They had tracked Jamie Mulholland all the way up the motorway, right to the parking place outside his flat. With every mile, Tanya became more and more disheartened. If he had been involved in murder, in the dismemberment of a body, then why would he be coming back from a trip abroad and heading for his own home?

By the time he had stepped from his van, rubbing at tired eyes, and then reached back to grab his bag from the passenger seat, a squad car and Tanya herself, with Paul in his own car as backup, had pulled in behind him.

His initial instinct appeared to be to turn and run. He glanced back and forth, and took a step away from the van. But with two burly officers and Paul Harris facing him, he realised that wasn't the way to go. He placed his bag on the ground beside him and faced them down.

"Alright, lads, take it easy." The Liverpool accent was more pronounced now, maybe the result of tiredness and tension.

Tanya stepped forward with her warrant card held high in front of her, though it was probably too dark for him to have any sort of real look at it. It didn't matter, he knew who she was from the occasion at the golf club. "Mr

Mulholland. We've been looking for you. I have to tell you that we had occasion to enter your home."

He stepped forward and she felt Paul Harris tense behind her, noticing the other officers lay hands on their tasers. She didn't want this to end in violence. She continued to speak. "We're still investigating the suspicious death at the golf club and, I don't know whether or not you are aware, but Mr Traynor has died as the result of a heart attack."

"Shit. What, Steve? Oh, bloody hell." He kicked at the ground in front of him, sparking up small pieces of gravel. That's – well…" He ran out of words.

"I'm sorry. There have been other developments and we were concerned for your wellbeing." It wasn't strictly true, but she hoped it might keep him calm.

"My wellbeing. Why the hell would you be bothered about me? I just work in the club."

"I wonder if we can have a look in your vehicle, sir?" As she spoke Tanya moved towards the white van.

Mulholland turned and slammed the door, plipped the key and thrust it into his pocket. "No."

"We're conducting a murder enquiry, Mr Mulholland. You don't really want to be obstructive." As he spoke, Paul had moved alongside Tanya. Now he pulled himself up to his full height, which was a good few inches taller than the other man. But Mulholland had learned well from his dealings with the Merseyside force and wasn't intimidated.

He looked Paul Harris up and down with a sneer. "Alright, mate, you come back with a warrant, you can have a look at my van. If you've done any damage to my place, I'll have you for it. Now, I'm tired, I'm going in." With that, he pushed passed and stormed off towards the apartment block.

There was nothing they could do. The search warrant had been for his flat, so the van was out of bounds. Tanya stepped up to the vehicle. There were no windows, the back doors were tightly locked and the whole exercise was a complete waste of their time.

She turned to Paul. "I want him watched. I want him followed."

"Right, boss. It's going to be a bit difficult with only me and DC Lewis."

"Bugger. Yes, of course it is. Look let's just keep an eye on his place here and track him if he goes off again on a jaunt. If he tries to leave the country, we could be able to hold him as a person of interest. I'll get on to the DCI, apply for a warrant to search this. If he carried either of the bodies in here, it'll light up like a firework display when we get the luminol and UV on it. Stay here for now, I'll come back in a couple of hours and take over, let you get home. If he leaves, let me know."

She could tell by his dour expression that it wasn't how Paul Harris had planned to spend the night, but she was so frustrated she had no sympathy. She would go home and have a shower, make a flask and some sandwiches to see her through the night and then come back. If the suspect had anything on his conscience that would drive him out into the cold drizzle, then she would know about it. There was just a CCTV image of the white van at the clubhouse in the days before the body was found and the other video of the same sort of vehicle driving towards the hut and away again. It was so little, but it was everything they had. She knew very well that it was the little things that eventually led to the big breaks. This was still worth following.

She stormed across the forecourt, turning as she reached her own car. She looked up through the orange glow of the streetlamp and saw the shape of Jamie Mulholland in his window, watching.

Chapter 50

It was after eight when Tanya relieved Paul Harris, by which time he was grumpy and cold. She pulled in at the kerb out of sight of the flats, flashed her headlights and waited until he walked back to slide into her car with a huff. "Sorry, Paul. I've been tied up trying to organise a warrant to search Mulholland's van. I think we're in with a chance but probably tomorrow. We might consider hauling him in for a chat, but I don't want to pre-empt things and make life difficult later. I brought you a burger and coke."

He took the fast food bag with a grunt of thanks. "So, back here tomorrow then?"

"Yes. But I'm going to hang around now, just in case. You get off though. Thanks."

"Can I ask you something, boss?" Paul said.

"Of course, what's up?"

"I've been sitting, thinking. Nothing else to do, was there?"

Tanya let him get away with the dig. She knew all too well how boring surveillance was, especially on your own.

"Why did Brian Finch not want me on his team? Don't get me wrong, I already said I think this is a more challenging case. But you know I thought we were getting on okay, him and me. I just wondered if it was some sort of reflection on my performance." He waited, picking at the lid of his drinks cup.

"He did want you. I had to fight for you. He wanted you and Kate. I wasn't having it. I told him that I needed you both." Tanya had to hide a smile as she saw the lift of Paul's head, the squaring of his shoulders. *Men and their egos.*

"Oh, right. So, he got the second string then?"

She sighed, no matter how often she told herself he was improving, he would soon let himself down with stupid comments.

"No, I got the team that would be of more use to me because of the way we'd been working. Anyway, if you've finished stinking up my car with that food, you can go. Back here tomorrow early. About seven."

"You're not staying all night, though?"

"I'll have to wait and see. If he just stays put, I suppose it'll serve me right. I've brought a blanket and a flask though. Go on, get off home to your poor wife."

"She's okay, she's got her mother staying."

It seemed that Paul and his wife spent very little time together as just the two of them. They hadn't been married long but they were sharing the early years with a lot of other people. Maybe this was the way that they could make it work. She hoped so, she hated to think of them adding to the long list of broken relationships. Again, she told herself it just wasn't worth taking the risk. Simon Hewitt was waiting for a call to arrange dinner – it was niggling at her. She had put him off in the restaurant, telling him that she was too focused on the case to be any sort of company, and he was patient and understanding. It made her feel guilty. It was just another thing that she would need to deal with. As Paul's car drew into the rain-swept road, she rubbed a hand over her face. It was so much easier when you didn't care about people. She had known that for a long time.

In the flat a shadow moved across the window, and the curtains twitched. Where Paul had been, on the main road outside the apartment block, the road was dry. But already the rain was darkening the tarmac. She saw Jamie Mulholland lean to the window and peer down into the darkness. So, he had known he was being watched. That was the trouble dealing with habitual criminals, they knew as much as the police did about procedure. She pulled away from the kerb and drove around the corner. If he had noticed her car then he might believe that she had left. She turned off her headlights and reversed across the junction where she parked on the forecourt of a boarded-up house. The entryway was muddy and full of weeds so there was little danger of it being used by the owners. From here she had a view of the road, his flat and his van. She slithered down in the seat and poured a cup of coffee, cursing as the steam clouded the car windows. She rubbed at them with a tissue.

After a couple of hours, the front door of the building opened and the dark figure of Mulholland stepped out, head bent against the chilly drizzle. The indicators flashed briefly as he approached his van but when he left the car park, he had not turned on his driving lights. She waited as long as she dared before pulling around the corner. She could just make out the ruby glow of his rear lights, both of them, as the van turned at the first junction.

She realised after just a few minutes that he was heading in the direction of the golf club. Tanya knew she should call for backup but didn't want to spook him with extra vehicles. She would follow him and when she had a better idea of what he was up to, then she would bring in help. If she needed it.

Chapter 51

There were a couple of cars in the car park. Through the window of the clubhouse, Tanya could see the drinkers, people for whom sitting behind the rain-soaked windows with a glass of wine or beer was more tempting than being in their own homes on this rainy, chilly evening. She knew there were meals served and wondered who oversaw the bar while Jamie Mulholland was off in France, or Spain, or wherever. She must check that they had been interviewed. With the death of the secretary it was possible that some staff members had been missed, people who were only there sporadically. She'd speak to Kate.

The white van pulled passed the parked cars and into the side alley where it had previously been picked up by CCTV. Jamie jumped down from the driving seat and disappeared around the corner of the building.

Tanya parked between two hulking Range Rovers. If Mulholland came back this way, she hoped he wouldn't notice her little car between the two juggernauts. If he did then she would deal with it; it was an open investigation, she could come up with a reason for her presence.

She crossed the gravelled area keeping as close as possible to the shadowed edges. She pulled up the hood on her jacket, partly to hide her face, but mainly because of the cold rain blown by a strengthening, peevish wind.

Pressed against the wall of the clubhouse, she peered into the alley where light from a storage unit spilled out and across the gravel. She could hear Jamie Mulholland moving around. When he left the unit to return to his van she pushed backwards, crouching between the sopping branches of some ornamental shrubs.

Jamie opened the rear doors of his truck, turned on a light inside and then vanished back into the storage unit. Tanya uncurled from her cold hiding place and ran the few steps to the vehicle. The cargo space was filled with boxes. Most of them were sealed with tape and secured with straps. She took out her phone and recorded a few images. She knew that she had no authorisation to be doing this, and it wasn't what she had been expecting. In truth, she couldn't have said what she really did expect. If the van floor had been marked with dark stains; if there had been blood splattered plastic sheeting; if there had been knives and tools that could be used to cut up a corpse, it would have been the find of a career. Instead, all she had was a van filled with – well with the stuff that a van should be filled with. Another blind alley. Another case of floundering in the dark and ending up with nothing.

She kicked out at the tyres and cursed her own ill-thought-out actions, turned away and stepped to the side of the van. That was when the world exploded in a flash of pain and the edges of her vision darkened as she slid into a heap on the puddled ground.

Chapter 52

There was pain, and noise, and a horrible swell of nausea. Tanya tried to open her eyes, but the light was too bright. Someone was patting at her hand and there was a voice, close to her ear, too loud. She batted at the presence.

"She's coming to. Get her a drink. Water, just water."

She heard a groan, realised it was herself, and cut it off. She was half sitting, half lying on a soft seat, but there was too much noise; a throbbing in her aching head. She lifted a hand and felt sticky warmth.

"It's alright, love, you're not bleeding much anymore. You'll be okay. We've sent for an ambulance. Here, take this." A glass was pressed to her lips and, as she swallowed the cold water, she forced her eyelids open.

A tall man bent over her, offering her the drink. Beside her, gripping her other hand sat a skinny woman – what her mother would have described as a gin woman: heavy make-up, garish, dangling earrings pulling at her lobes, and a tight leopard skin top. She leaned closer and Tanya smelled booze and garlic; the nausea threatened again.

"Keep still, bab. You've had an accident."

She knew it sounded ridiculous and as the words left her lips, she wanted to bite them back. "Where am I? Who are you? What happened?"

She pushed more upright on the settee, reached out and took the glass of water into her hand. She smiled up at the tall bloke, leaned away from the garlic breath of his companion. In the background was a crowd of interested spectators. She knew now where she was. The inside of the club room was warm, it smelled of food, and perfume, and wet clothes.

"What happened?" she asked again.

"Well, love." Gin woman shook her head. "We don't know. Bob here –" she pointed at the man who had given her the water "– he went out to bring the car round to the door and you were flat out on the ground. Wet through in the rain. You're all muddy, look." She pointed at Tanya's rain-soaked trousers which were smeared with mud and marks from the gravel.

Her brain was clearing and though her head pounded, she was managing to think more logically. She peered into the little group who were watching the drama. Jamie Mulholland wasn't one of them. She leaned a little to the side to look past, but he wasn't behind the bar either. A young woman was polishing a glass as she stared across the room, eyes wide, enjoying the fuss. There was a man in kitchen whites, a check kerchief over his hair, who stood in a doorway to the side. Tanya searched her pounding head for the last thing she could remember. She had followed the club manager to the car park, she knew that. Then there was nothing. Had she confronted him? She couldn't recall.

"Does anyone have any idea what happened to me?" She felt pathetic asking yet again for information, but there was a gap in her memory, and she needed to fill it quickly.

The man called Bob spoke. "I think you might have been hit by a branch, love. It's pretty windy out there, and there are bits of tree all over the car park. I didn't take that much notice, to be honest. The weather has turned really nasty and I just wanted to get you inside."

"Thank you." Tanya smiled at him. "But was there no van?"

"No love, nothing. You were over in the gap between the clubhouse and the pro shop. It was just luck that I saw you. There's no parking over there. We think your car is in the area by the hedge. Did you put it next to a silver Discovery? Can you remember?"

"I think so. Yes, that's probably mine. A small blue one."

"Aye, that'll be it. Listen here comes the ambulance now. They'll see you right."

"Oh, no. No, I don't want an ambulance. I'm fine really."

"Well, it's too late." The woman moved to stand from the seat beside her and Tanya caught a faint whiff of body odour. It really didn't help. "Can you remember your name?"

"Yes, of course. Yes." She pushed a hand into her pocket and pulled out her warrant card, flipped it open and held it up. "That's me. Detective Inspector Miller, and I'm fine. Thank you."

"Oh right. I thought I recognised her." This from one of the secondary watchers. "She was here about that body. The one in the shed. She's the one who tried to help Steve. Used the defibrillator and what have you."

The mumbling became white noise as Tanya closed her eyes and fought to remember.

* * *

It took a while, but she managed to convince the paramedics that she didn't need to be taken to the hospital. They stuck a couple of Steristrips on her injured head and made her promise to see her own doctor in the morning, and report to A&E immediately if the dizziness and nausea returned or worsened.

Nobody was happy with the idea of her driving. She knew that if an emergency ambulance had been called then a police car would be on the way and she could wait for them and have them take her home. She didn't think they'd be rushing though, and she just wanted to get away from the muggy clubhouse. She needed peace and quiet and room to think. In the end, she agreed to take a taxi and left the car to be collected.

* * *

Back in her own house she stuffed the filthy, wet clothes into the washing machine and wrapped herself in a fluffy dressing gown. Against all advice, she poured a glass of whisky, settled back on the settee in the dim room and tried to make sense of what had happened.

She called Paul Harris. He answered after a few rings, but she could tell he was groggy from sleep. She gave him a brief precis of the events since he had left her at the block of flats. "I'm just beginning to function properly again," she said. "I still feel a bit foggy, but we need to take action now. I know I should have bloody organised it already, but it was all so confusing. Get a watch out for him. Have a squad car sent to his flat. I don't know what happened to me, I really don't, but I don't believe I was hit by a tree branch."

"Are you sure you shouldn't be at the hospital?" Paul asked.

"Probably, but I can't stand those places, and this is a development. I've taken some painkillers for my headache, but they haven't kicked in yet. Please, Sergeant, sort the alert for his van for me. I'll catch a few hours sleep and then see you in the office. It's…" She glanced at her watch. "Just after midnight. Let's get into work about six in the morning. We'll regroup there. Call Kate at a more reasonable hour, will you? Bring her up to date. God, I just need to have a lie down, just for a bit."

"I don't think there's any point in searching his flat again, but we need someone out there to watch for him. We have a solid reason now to bring him in; when we find him. I reckon he must have clobbered me. It's the only explanation I can come up with. Damn it, I wish I could remember," Tanya continued.

"Don't stress, boss. I'll get an all points alert sorted and I'll pick you up around six. I assume you didn't drive home?"

"Bugger, no I didn't. We'll need to send someone to fetch my car in the morning. What a bloody mess."

Chapter 53

Tanya slept. When she woke it was to a pounding headache and sweeping nausea as she lifted her head from the pillow. Her hair was knotted and sticky with dried blood. The paramedics had told her to keep the area dry but there was no way she was turning up at work with her hair clogged and filthy. She stuck a second dressing over the first and managed a reasonable job with it all in the shower. When she pulled the sticking plaster away it dragged hairs from her scalp and the pain brought tears to her eyes. She felt battered, woozy and sore but had to press through it.

She couldn't face food, but two cups of strong coffee helped and by the time Paul Harris blew the horn outside she was functioning at least.

"They've found him."

She had barely fastened her seat belt before Harris blurted out the news, grinning at her as he pulled away from the kerb.

"Excellent, where?"

"M6, on his way up north. I reckon he was heading for home, like a rat scurrying for his hiding place. They're bringing him back. They've impounded the van, and now we have a clear reason to examine it. It was filled with booze and cigarettes, but he's given no explanation. He hasn't said anything, just asked for a solicitor. He's well practised in all this, isn't he?"

"He is, but it won't matter if we find something in his van to link him to our bodies."

"Or something to prove he gave you that egg on your head."

Tanya touched the sore spot tenderly, she winced. "How does it look?"

"Like you've been clouted with a heavy object. You look a bit off actually, boss."

"Yes, I know, but I think I look worse than I feel. Now we've got Mulholland I reckon we're on the way." Although she had managed to sound upbeat and confident, she mentally crossed her fingers because so much of this was supposition and hope.

* * *

They left Jamie Mulholland sitting in an interview room on his own for a couple of hours. He looked tired and bored. He asked for coffee, breakfast, and a legal representative. The duty solicitor was called and when he came there was the inevitable "No comment. Nothing to say." It went back and forth for a while and it was no more than they had expected. Tanya let Paul Harris and Kate Lewis handle it. She drank more coffee and brought the DCI up to date with the developments.

It was a long morning and she felt more and more ill as the hours passed. By lunchtime, her vision was blurring, and she admitted to herself that she really ought to have some medical attention for what was obviously concussion. But she couldn't go, not now, not when they were getting somewhere. She called the team examining the van over and over until in the end, the sergeant in charge pointed out that they would be able to get on with it all much quicker if she would leave them to do their jobs.

"We've got boxes of booze and fags," he told her, "a few tools, not much more than that. I've sent a big spanner off already because there was some hair and blood on it. From what I've heard that could be yours, Detective Inspector, so you'll have him. But apart from that, we're still working on it. Why don't you find someone else to torment, eh?"

She could have put him on report for his attitude, but she needed him on her side and truthfully, she had to acknowledge he had a point.

She walked down the corridor and watched in frustration from the viewing room while Kate and Paul got nowhere with the interview. She was relieved by the distraction when her phone rang and she saw Simon Hewitt's name on the screen.

"Tanya, I heard you were hurt; are you okay?"

"Not really, to be honest, but it'll help when I get this scrote locked up."

"Has he admitted anything, yet?" Hewitt asked.

"No, but they've found evidence in his van. Not the stuff I was hoping for, but they're still working on it." She wanted him to go away now, it made her head pound just to talk.

"Well, look, be careful. You really should see someone. You've probably got concussion and you can't mess about with that."

"Yes, I know. I'll see the doctor later." She moved her finger to finish the call.

"There is just one other thing, Tanya."

She closed her eyes and waited in silence for him to continue.

"We've had the toxicology report on the suicide… Mr Baker."

It wasn't what she had been expecting and, as she made the mistake of shaking her head in confusion, fireworks exploded inside her skull. She groaned.

"Are you okay. You really shouldn't be in work. Won't you go home?" Hewitt said.

"I'm fine. You were telling me about Baker."

"Yes. We knew that there would be drugs in his system; I think a glass was found at the scene, there was residue."

"That's right. He must have taken something and then settled into the car and let the fumes do the rest."

"Well, that's logical. We found evidence of the anti-anxiolytic that he'd been prescribed. There was something else though. I had them double check before I called you."

She needed to sit down, she really wished he'd get on with it. "What else was there?"

"There was ketamine and cocaine. Enough to knock out a horse."

"Bloody hell, really? Well, he meant to do a good job didn't he?"

Dr Hewitt hadn't finished. "With the new information, I had them go back and have another look at his body."

Tanya felt the throb in her head as her heart pounded. There was something here, something important. She wanted to scream at him to get to the point. She pulled a chair away from the wall, lowering herself carefully into the plastic seat. "Yes, and?"

"There is a needle mark on his left arm. Nobody had looked for it because it seemed that we understood what had happened to him – sloppy work and I shall be having a word. I should have supervised more closely; the new examiner is still fairly inexperienced. She's feeling bad now, so she'll have learned from it, but the buck has to stop with me. Anyway, that's my problem, well mine and my staff's, but there will be a full enquiry, the results will be disclosed. I would say he took some of the drug by mouth, there was evidence of it in his stomach. He has a broken tooth. There's no way to know for certain when that happened, but the rest of his dental work is well maintained."

"What does that mean?" Tanya asked.

"Well, it suggests to me that he was forcibly made to swallow the drugs in the glass and his tooth was damaged in the process. That was probably done to try and convince us it was suicide. We will now re-examine his stomach contents, in case the piece of tooth is there. But he could have spat it out. Once he was subdued, then the heavy sedation was administered by injection. It's still a vague possibility that he did that himself but there was no syringe, no tourniquet in the car. I took the liberty of reading the report before I called you."

"Could he have done it in the house and then walked to the car?"

"I would say, no. With the prescribed drugs yes, but not with the injected substance."

"Then the only explanation…" Tanya paused.

"Yes, the only viable explanation is that there was a third party involved." Simon Hewitt was speaking quietly now.

"Bloody hell. He was murdered and it was set up to look like a suicide."

"I'm afraid it looks like it, Detective Inspector. I'm ashamed to say that it almost worked."

Tanya slid her phone onto the table and lowered her head onto her crossed arms. She should have made reassuring noises, tried to make him feel better. But she just needed to think straight, she really did, and the pounding in her head, the nausea, was getting in the way. She'd have more coffee.

Chapter 54

A few minutes in the quiet of her office helped. Tanya popped some more painkillers, they weren't helping much. She knew it was too soon, but the thunder in her head wouldn't let her think, and she really needed to think.

She heard Detectives Harris and Lewis in the incident room and dragged herself down the corridor. When Kate Lewis saw her, she screwed up her face. "Ma'am, you really should be at home, or better still at the hospital – you look terrible." As she spoke, she pulled a chair from beneath one of the desks and Tanya sank into it.

Kate continued, "Mulholland and his solicitor have demanded a break. We still haven't got very far, but we haven't told him about the spanner in his van. Once we reveal that, I reckon he'll see the sense in talking. He must know it was there. I suppose he's been hoping we'll overlook it. We're saving it until confirmation comes back from the lab, so he has no wiggle room."

"Okay, keep pegging away at him. But I've had a call from Dr Hewitt." She told them the latest development.

"That doesn't fit with anything," Paul Harris said.

"I know. It's another complication. Thing is though, there is a connection between Mulholland and Baker, isn't there; it's only slight but they did know each other at the golf club."

"Do you fancy him for murder though?" Kate said "Why? Unless Baker really knew more than he told us, and Mulholland was threatened by it. Possible, I suppose. I know you can't really go by appearances, but I just don't feel it, to be honest."

"Well, he could have finished me off if he'd hit me a bit harder," Tanya said. "To be honest, the way I feel right now I almost wish he had." She laughed at the look on their faces. "Okay, poor taste. Sorry."

"It's a bloody tangled sort of a carry on though, isn't it?" Paul said.

"Yes, I think we need to have a meeting and get everything straightened out – update the book, sort the boards. There have been developments now and we really have to keep it all straight. We need ideas as much as anything, and I don't need to tell you that we need them now." She looked up as a uniformed officer appeared in the doorway.

"Detective Inspector Miller?" she said.

"Me." Tanya held up a hand.

"There's a PCSO in reception, she's insisting on speaking to you. Says she has information about the body in the lake. The female murder victim."

"What's her name?"

"Karen Laidlaw. She's a youngster, but very insistent."

"Okay, I'll speak to her. Bring her up here, will you? Kate, can you sort the boards with the new information, and then let me know when you go back down to the interview? Paul get on to the lab, see where they are at with the spanner. They should have a blood group by now and if they want some hair for comparison, they can send someone up. They have my DNA on record already, though that won't help immediately."

* * *

Karen Laidlaw was in uniform and doing her best not to be overawed by her surroundings. On another day Tanya might have been more welcoming, suggesting the woman have a look at the incident room, answering any questions she might have. Although she thought the PCSOs were lacking in ambition, taking an easy route to being in uniform, she would always encourage a young woman. She might even have suggested the girl think about taking the next step and applying to join the main force. Today, though, she just wanted her to say her piece and then leave her in the quiet and think.

"You have something for me, Officer Laidlaw?"

"Yes. At least I think I have, it's not much, well it could be, but it needs to be looked into. I tried to get the sergeant to do something, but it was too late, and he just said that someone else would probably handle it."

Tanya held up a hand. "Okay, officer. Just take a breath and try to make some sense. Nothing of what you have just said has told me anything." She knew she sounded cranky, but that was how she felt, and this didn't seem as though it was going anywhere.

"Sorry, ma'am." Laidlaw hesitated a moment and gathered her thoughts. "We've had a young woman in custody. She was involved in a mugging; she stole a mobile phone. She refused to speak even though we had her for a couple of days. We know she isn't English, but that's all. Eventually we had to hand her over to the immigration people. Even though she may be here legally, she made no attempt to answer questions that would have saved her being held and perhaps deported."

"Where are you going with this?" Tanya struggled with rising impatience.

"Sorry, I just wanted to give you a bit of background, ma'am. Anyway, as she was being transported, she spotted this." Karen held up the poster showing the computer-generated image of the female victim. "She said that this woman was her friend and asked me to let her know where they were taking her. It was too late for me to ask her anything, they had her in the van before I had a chance. Then, of course, I found out that this is one of your murder victims."

"Bloody hell, officer, why didn't you just say? Kate, get in here." Tanya made the mistake of standing too quickly and shouting through to the incident room. The floor tipped, and her stomach churned. She leaned against the desk. "Detective Lewis take Officer Laidlaw and get as many details as you can from her. There is a young woman being held by immigration who can identify our Jane Doe. Get on it, will you."

The two women left and as the door closed behind them Tanya slid to the floor of her office with a soft thud.

Chapter 55

This time when she awoke, Tanya knew immediately where she was. She recognised the posters on the wall, the pale green paint, and the thin, hard bed that she was lying on. She knew that when she turned her head, Sister Rouse would be sitting behind the desk. The senior nurse practitioner administered anti-tetanus injections, dressed wounds, and decided who did and did not need to be sent to the hospital, all with the same dour expression and cold manner. Years of dealing with antsy detainees and argumentative officers had soured whatever bedside manner she might have had.

"Ah, Detective Inspector, you've decided to re-join us." The thin woman in an unflattering trouser suit uniform, grabbed Tanya's wrist to take her pulse. She shone a light into her eyes. "You've been stupid. You should have been at the hospital. You do know that I am risking the wrath of the DCI by having you in here. We should have stuck you straight in an ambulance when we scraped you off the floor of your office."

Tanya didn't answer; she could tell there was more to come.

"Promise me you'll go home, now, have a friend to stay with you tonight, and take at least three days sick. It should be longer, but I am aware that you are in the middle of something and we are so thin on the ground you probably wouldn't stick to it anyway. I'm not in the habit of wasting breath."

"I'm okay. Got a headache, obviously, but I think I just needed some food. I didn't have breakfast." Tanya knew that she wasn't going to get away with it.

Sister Rouse didn't even bother to argue. "There's a leaflet here. Read it; it tells you what to watch out for. Any of these symptoms, don't mess about – get medical care. Now, either agree or I'm having you taken to the hospital immediately."

There was no choice and while she waited for Kate Lewis to collect her Tanya read the leaflet, stuffed it into her pocket, and planned how much she would reasonably be able to achieve from home. Though she was frustrated and angry with herself, she had to admit that the thought of her quiet living room and the comfort of home was appealing.

* * *

"Do you want anything?" Kate had driven her home and now stood in the narrow hallway, not sure how to behave.

"Yes."

The straightforward response pleased her, and she stepped towards the kitchen, anticipating making tea and toast or bringing cushions and blankets from the bedroom.

"I want copies of everything we have. Send me an image of the boards. My occurrence book is in my briefcase, I'll need that. I need a secure link between us, and you need to keep me up to date constantly."

"Ma'am, Sister Rouse said rest – you're on the sick."

Tanya simply shook her head. It was a mistake. She groaned and laid a hand over her eyes. "I'll be okay here. I can rest if I need to, but you know I have to stay on this. It's started to come together. If I don't keep on top of it, DCI Scunthorpe will have no option but to hand it over to someone else, probably DI Finch. I'm not having it."

"But Sister Rouse will have made a report."

"That's why I need you to cover for me. If you have any problems from Scunthorpe's office, you need to make it look as though I'm toeing the line."

"But, ma'am, if anything happens to you…"

"Nothing is happening to me. Not if I can keep on top of all this. Oh yes, and Kate, please don't worry about staying. It's kind of you to offer but really, you should be at home, and you also need to be available in case we have to act quickly."

"I was supposed to stay, ma'am."

"I'll ring you a couple of times, just to let you know I'm okay. If anything happens that worries me, I'll let you know. No offence, Kate, but really, I would prefer to be on my own. I've only just got my house back to myself. Sorry if that sounds rude."

"No, I understand, ma'am, I do. Do you promise you won't do anything dodgy?"

"I promise. Now let's get things set up. I can work in the living room, that way I can have a break in comfort, if I need it."

"Well, at least let me make you some tea and toast."

"Oh, go on then. Thanks."

* * *

"Have you heard how the other investigation is going, Kate?" Tanya put her empty cup and plate back on the tray.

"Well, it hasn't been as cut and dried as everyone thought, apparently. According to Dan Price, they haven't been able to identify the woman."

"Hmm, that's interesting. Another Jane Doe turning up. Tell you what, keep in touch with Dan Price. Is that okay? I don't want to put you in a difficult position. Probably best not to mention much to Detective Constable Rollinson, she may feel her loyalties a bit – erm – stretched."

Kate smiled back at Tanya's choice of words. "It's fine, ma'am. Dave and me often meet for a coffee or lunch. He's a lovely bloke, young enough to be my son, I know, but we're mates."

"Okay, back to our own case. Let me know as soon as we hear anything from the immigration people. I want you to be ready to go and interview this witness, as soon as we find out where she is. I really hope it's not too late. If they've shipped her out already it's going to get terribly complicated. If I thought it would do any good, I'd have that sergeant hauled over the coals but really, what's the bloody point. We are all working ourselves to death and if you can slope your shoulders now and then, well…"

Kate gathered up her belongings and, much against her better judgement, prepared to leave Tanya, an officer whose shoulders were never going to slope.

Tanya was still not finished. "I need to go and speak to Mrs Baker. I don't want to pass it off onto anyone else. So, for now, we can't let this latest information about her husband get out. I'm hoping that by tomorrow afternoon I'll be up to it."

"Oh, boss. Sister Rouse'll crucify me."

"I'll take full responsibility; and think about it: if someone you cared about had been murdered, you'd expect to be told about it pretty bloody quickly, wouldn't you? We've already missed any chance of securing the place properly as a crime scene, but she needs to have a liaison officer assigned. It should be today but let's plan on tomorrow. We haven't had anything in writing from the morgue, so we should be able to muddy the water a bit. In fact, would you do that as well? Explain to Dr Hewitt and ask him to slow down on his report, play the sympathy card if you need to. Tell him I want to visit the widow in person but I'm not up to it right now."

Tanya continued, "It's not far and you can come with me. I'll be fine. Pick me up early afternoon. Thanks, Kate. You've been great, but you know what? I reckon right now I could use a bit of a sleep. I'll be in touch later and we'll see where we're at. Keep pegging away at Mulholland and let me know as soon as you break him. You will, you and Sergeant Harris. You will."

Chapter 56

She slept for more than three hours. The lights in the lounge were on timers and when the room suddenly brightened, Tanya jolted awake. Her neck was stiff and her feet cold, but she felt better. The pain in her head was a dull background ache, but her vision was clear and steady.

She leaned from the settee and dragged her laptop across the coffee table. When she swished a finger over the touch pad, there were messages from Kate and one from Simon Hewitt. She knew that once she started reading there would be action to take and responses required. She needed to pee and wanted a shower. She wanted to get into softer trousers and a warm hoody. For a minute she was torn but, in the end, went upstairs by way of the kitchen, where she stopped to turn on the coffee maker and put a couple of waffles into the toaster.

Once she was clean, comfortable and with a hot drink, and some stodgy snacks, she was ready to work. With luck, this was the beginning of the end.

The message from Simon was a mixture of concern and information. He offered to come to her home with whatever she needed. He offered to stay, or to have one of his female members of staff move in overnight. She grimaced at the thought of strangers babysitting her, but the thought of Simon in her home, taking care of her in his quiet way wasn't awful. She wouldn't accept, but it wasn't awful.

The rest of the message was in response to a request from Kate to keep them informed about Finch's case – the graveyard body. Tanya was impressed that the detective constable had taken the initiative. Dr Hewitt was aware of the situation between Tanya and Brian Finch and he would be discreet. As far as anyone knew the two cases were unconnected but Tanya felt instinctively that they should follow developments.

At first, the news about Mulholland made her smile. Once he was told that they had matched the hair and blood to Tanya, once they stressed that they had irrefutable evidence of his assault on her and she was now very ill and there was grave concern for her wellbeing – Kate had posted a grinning emoticon beside the comment – then he had admitted that yes, he had been responsible for the attack.

> *'He tried to say he hadn't known who you were boss and thought someone was nicking stuff from his van. But when he realised, he was probably going down for it, we helped him to see the sense in coming clean. I've got his full statement and it's interesting reading, I've attached a copy. I need to tell you though, it's probably not what you want to hear – or see in this case.'*

Kate signed off with an arrangement for either herself or Paul Harris to collect Tanya the next afternoon to take her to see Patricia Baker.

The coffee went cold in the cup as Tanya read the statement and as she did so, her heart sank with disappointment. She had been so very sure that they were about to get to the heart of the thing.

The electronic copy of his statement showed the force logo, the headings that she had expected and when she scrolled to the end there was his signature. She skimmed the preliminaries and then read the pertinent sections a couple of times, looking for anything that might give her a reason to hope that it hadn't all been misdirection. There was nothing.

... I drove to the golf club. I went into the store room and when I came back outside, I saw there was someone interfering in the back of the van. There was a load of money tied up in that cargo. Wine, spirits, fags. I thought it was somebody trying to nick stuff. I didn't know it was a police officer and I certainly didn't know it was a woman. I'm sorry I hit her. I hope she's okay.

I bought the stuff in France and Spain. I've been doing it for a while now. Me and Steve – Steven Traynor – the secretary of the golf club, had a thing going. We got the stuff cheap, sold it in the club full price and we didn't report it anywhere. The money went into our pockets, we split it fifty-fifty. We've been doing it for about eighteen months. I didn't think there was any harm in it. Those rich bastards can afford it.

I didn't know Steve had died. I was in France. When I found out I didn't know what to do but I just thought I'd carry on. Until there was a new secretary it would have been okay, and I could have kept all the money.

After the body was found in that hut, Steve – Mr Traynor – was panicked and wanted to stop. He was scared the filth was hanging around and thought we'd get caught. I had tried to tell him they wouldn't be looking at us, but he was a bit of a wuss. Anyway, maybe that's why he had the heart attack, I don't know. Nothing to do with me that.

I don't know anything about the poor sod in the hut, I've never even been in it. I don't play golf – that's for the nobs. I've only played a round once and I was shit at it.

If the police woman had kept her nose out, none of this would have happened so it's not my fault is it ...

Tanya lay on the settee and closed her eyes. They were back to square one. All the time and energy she had spent, all the hope – it had been about smuggled booze and some pathetic side-line. Tears trickled from under her lids and she pushed up wearily from the settee.

She reached out to call Kate Lewis and before she dialled realised that there was nothing to say. It was over and now it was up to the CPS to decide whether to prosecute. At that moment, the idea of Jamie Mulholland in the dock was small comfort, and the idea of having to explain it all in court was ghastly. She had been acting on her own, that was wrong. She didn't have a warrant, that was wrong. It had all been a massive misdirection, that was wrong. There was so much wrong with what they'd done that it was a real possibility the case would fail. Even the assault would be weak as she had been working alone and hadn't gone down official channels. He would more than likely walk away. She was livid with herself, with him and with the system. There was nothing more to do right now than to go to bed.

She did eventually manage to sleep. Her dreams were tormented. Over and over she chased unreachable enemies down endless roads on limbs that couldn't carry her fast enough. Over and over she came just close enough to grasp at fading, indistinct figures, only to watch them vanish and reappear further away. She was glad when her alarm sounded, and she could drag herself from the wrinkled bed.

* * *

There was a new suit in her dressing room, a pair of shoes she had only worn once and some new underwear still in the tissue paper wrapping. New things always made her feel better, there had been so few of them in the past.

She had a shower, spritzed herself with some Joy perfume and took her laptop into her small office. She stood for a minute in front of the mirror. The new outfit looked good. There were still dark shadows under her eyes, her hair didn't look right where her scalp was swollen but she stared at her reflection. The face looking back was hard and honest.

She thought of the rotting corpse in the hut; the sad, soaked, woman's body abandoned in the pond; and the ghastly limbs and skull thrown like trash in woodland. They needed her to let go of the self-pity. They demanded the best that she could do. She straightened her shoulders and turned to her desk, opened her files, and went back to the beginning.

She worked for a solid couple of hours, scribbling notes on the pad beside her and highlighting points on the screen.

She rang Kate. "Have you found that missing immigrant woman?"

"Yes, ma'am. She's being held at Colnburn. I'm waiting for a call back to let me know when I can interview her. Should be this afternoon."

"Right. I'm coming with you. I want you to pick me up as soon as you can. We need to get moving; this has all gone tits up and it's my fault. Get on to the morgue and ask for a viewable image of the woman in DI Finch's case. Only speak to Dr Hewitt. There are bodies turning up everywhere, we've got our two, the graveyard girl and Peter Baker. All in a small area. All in a short space of time. We need to look for connections."

"But, boss, they're all different."

"No, they're not. They're all dead is what they are. Get a copy of the post-mortem report for Finch's case. Quick as you can. I've been a bloody fool, and this is all coming back to bite us on the bum. Baker's house first and then on to Colnburn. If they haven't got back to you, we'll blag our way in. Oh yes, tell Detective Sergeant Harris to fix the boards while we're gone. Do you think he'll be able to do that without cocking it up?"

"Yes, ma'am. I'll give him a quick briefing."

For the next half hour, Tanya paced back and forth along the hallway, peering outside now and then, as if just looking would bring Kate's car down the road more quickly. She swallowed some painkillers and drank more coffee, but adrenaline had done more for her than medicine and caffeine and the idea that the case was slipping away had energised her. She was buzzing.

Chapter 57

Tricia Baker was dressed in black from head to foot. She looked stylish and poised. Her brother was at the house when they arrived and took a seat on the settee next to his sister. He wrapped an arm around her shoulders briefly.

The widow initiated the conversation. "I assume you are here to tell me that I can have his body now. I need to arrange things. My husband had many friends, we are planning a quiet funeral and cremation and then a memorial service. We can't do any of it until you let me have him. There are things that need to be sorted out at the office, I can't concentrate on any of that until things get back to normal."

Tanya wondered about the reference to a normal life when it would forever be without her husband. She let it go, the woman was grieving. She took a breath and shook her head. All designed to prepare them for news that they would not want to hear.

"I'm afraid, Mrs Baker, that there will be more delay."

It was Robin Turner who exploded. "Don't be bloody ridiculous. How long are we supposed to put up with this? This is torture for my sister. How can she be expected to move on? I shall have a word, I have contacts. This is totally unacceptable, Detective Inspector."

It was no more than they had expected. Tanya and Kate sat quietly until he regained some composure.

"There has been a further development I'm afraid. I have some upsetting news for you, Mrs Baker," Tanya said. "Further to the post-mortem and toxicology results from the lab, I have to tell you that it would appear there was a third party involved in your husband's death. I am so very sorry. We will arrange for a family liaison officer to be assigned. We will work as quickly as we can and keep you informed at all times. We will need to examine the garage and car again. We will need access to his room, and anything that you can tell us about his business contacts, or indeed anyone with whom he may have had disagreements. All of that will help to move things along more quickly."

Tanya waited for the tears and the disbelief. The fury was unexpected.

Patricia Baker shook with anger as she stood from the settee. "Don't be so bloody ridiculous. What on earth are you talking about? A third party. What third party? Get out, get out and take care of your business. Let me have my husband's body back, or I can promise you, Detective Inspector there will be repercussions."

At first, they thought that she had misunderstood and although they had tried to be gentle, Tanya saw that she needed to be more straightforward. "Mrs Baker, what I am telling you now is that your husband was most probably unlawfully killed. Do you understand me?"

"Ridiculous," Tricia Baker said. She turned to her brother who now stood beside her. "Robin. Make them leave. Do something."

"Mrs Baker. Please try to calm down. I understand that this must be a terrible shock, but there are things that we need to do now. There are questions that we must ask you. We will do all that we can to find who did this terrible thing, but really, I must ask you to calm down. Would you like a glass of water?" As Tanya spoke, she nodded at Kate Lewis who prepared to go into the kitchen and fetch a drink.

"No. I don't want a bloody drink of water. I want you to leave, take your horrible suspicions and filthy lies, and leave."

There was a real risk that the woman was about to become hysterical and it was obvious this wasn't the time for questions. Robin Turner had wrapped his sister in his arms and led her back to the settee. He murmured calming words.

"We'll come back later. I'm afraid there is no choice. Mr Turner, it may be a good idea to call your sister's doctor," Tanya said.

"I don't need your advice, thank you and please ring before you come back here. In the meantime, I am going to make some calls. This is unforgivable."

Back in the car Tanya and Kate sat in silence for a while. The outburst had shaken both of them. "Poor woman," Kate said.

"Hmm. Nasty shock for her. We'll have to come back though. I don't care how many contacts they have and who they can call, we need to speak to her again."

Chapter 58

On the way to Colnburn Detention Centre's women's unit, where a couple of dozen females were held, Kate received a text confirming the interview. They showed their IDs but didn't need to have their fingerprints or photographs taken. They signed the log. They left their personal stuff locked in the car boot in preference to leaving them in lockers in the reception area. Once through the metal detector, they were led to a visitors' room.

The girl waiting to speak to them was pale and thin. She had dark rings under her eyes, which were puffy and red. They were told she was still refusing to say anything about where she was from, what family she had or anything that would help them to decide what would be the best thing for her. She didn't mix with the other detainees, and they were seriously concerned for her mental health. She had told them her name was Ana but beyond that she was mute.

"We have tried to explain to her that as they are not going to prosecute on the minor robbery, and providing she is from an EU country then, at least for the moment, she has done nothing wrong." The female immigration officer seemed genuinely caring and frustrated by the problem. "It's done no good; she's scared of something, that's what I reckon. She's been fed some sort of tale to keep her quiet and we're getting nowhere. I hope you have some luck with her." She left them facing each other in the bare room in the silence.

"She seems nice," Kate said. "Things must have improved here lately, it had some bad press back in the day.

"Are you being treated well?" Tanya asked the girl. There was no response.

Tanya slid the printed image of their female victim out of the cardboard folder. She placed it upside down on the table between them. "Ana, is it okay if I call you Ana?"

There was no response.

"I've been speaking to one of the PCSOs, the woman who was there when you stole the phone." There was a flash of panic in the other woman's eyes and Tanya raised a hand trying to calm her.

"It's alright, we're not here about that. That's all over. But Karen…" She stuck to Christian names in an effort to diffuse the tension. "Karen told me that when you were leaving the police station you saw a picture of someone you think you know."

The use of the present tense was deliberate and as Ana raised her eyes, the hope in them was heart-breaking.

As she turned the picture over, for just a moment, Tanya hated her job. "Do you know who this is, Ana?"

The days of being silent had made the woman's voice croaky, but she reached out to lift the picture as her eyes filled with tears. "My friend. She is my friend. She went to London. Please, will you tell her where I am? Will you ask her to help me?"

There was a beat while Tanya considered her response. She felt much more sympathy for this woman than she had for the angry widow of the morning, but the truth had to come out.

"I'm very sorry, Ana. Your friend won't be able to help you. I'm afraid she is dead." There was nothing else she could say. All they could do was witness the devastation on the face of the woman sitting opposite them.

Ana raised a hand to cover her streaming eyes, she was sobbing uncontrollably. They waited until she calmed a little. They knew what the next question would be, and knew they were about to add to the distress. It was unavoidable. Tanya turned towards Kate and wasn't terribly surprised to see the glint of tears in the officer's eyes. She was a kind, motherly woman and would be feeling dreadful.

"Why is she dead?" The incorrect English added a poignant note to the terrible question, but they knew what she was asking.

"She was killed, Ana. I'm sorry but someone killed your friend."

"Not Elian. Elian would not. He was simple and innocent. He would not. Can I speak to Elian?" She paused, horrified, and then spoke in a whisper, "Elian is dead as well. We were all warned. I know he is dead also."

Tanya and Kate glanced at each other. They both felt it – the case had just split wide open.

Chapter 59

In sobbing gulps, Ana told them about her friend Dani. That they had lived and worked together, somewhere in England. She would not tell them where. She told them about Elian, the young man who had also run away when Dani left. She refused to give them any information about where they had been held, simply that they worked for an agency, that they owed money, and until the debt was paid there was no way out.

She told them that they were all afraid and unhappy, but no matter how hard they pushed she refused to give them any more names or locations. Just that there was a damp and dirty house, caravans, a factory, and endless work every day. She explained that she had been desperate to call home – that was why she needed the phone. She stopped and then asked that they tell the old woman that she was sorry she'd been hurt. These things came out in stops and starts and she constantly fell back into the silence, shaking her head. Reassurances from Tanya that they would take care of her and her family did nothing to break through the wall of fear. She held the picture of her dead friend, pressing it to her chest, and breaking into more heart-rending sobs each time she glanced at it.

The officer in charge of the unit intervened when her sobs became so overwhelming that she was gasping for breath. A doctor was called. Despite Tanya's pleas, they administered a sedative. There was now no option but for them to return the next day when the girl had come to terms with the news and might be more help to them.

As they led her from the room, already heavy-eyed and sluggish, Tanya pulled the image of the girl who had been found in the graveyard from the folder. "I'm sorry, I'm really sorry, Ana. Do you know who this is?" They hadn't told her that this woman was also dead but there was no need – she connected the dots immediately.

The cry of anguish told them everything they needed to know.

"Emilia. Is Emilia. Is my fault. Is all my fault." With the final declaration, the woman collapsed to the floor in a semi-conscious daze and had to be taken from the room in a wheelchair.

Tanya and Kate Lewis sat in the car gulping cold water from a bottle. "God, that was ghastly," Kate murmured. "How did you know, boss?"

"What?"

"How did you know to show her the picture of Finch's victim?"

"I don't know, I really don't, well not enough to explain it anyway. It was just a feeling. Too many bodies, too many coincidences. We'll come back tomorrow, get what we can, but we've got to move ourselves. We have to find out where they were being held. When she's had time to reflect and, hopefully, started to get angry and see that she owes her friends some justice, well, maybe that'll encourage her to tell us. I hope so, because if she goes back to not speaking it's going to get very unpleasant for us all. This isn't fun, is it, Kate?"

"No, ma'am, it's not. The job is hard a lot of the time but now and then it all just seems too hard. We just keep going though, don't we? We have to get to the truth, no matter how horrible. I wish we could do it without hurting that poor girl any more though."

"Yes."

They drove away between the tall metal fences and, until Tanya's phone beeped, they could think of nothing to say.

Kate picked up the handset and read the text message. "Hmm, I reckon we might be in trouble, boss. DCI Scunthorpe wants you in his office as soon as possible. He wants an estimated time of arrival. Sister Rouse must have heard what we've done."

"I'll take full responsibility, Kate. I'll let them know I didn't give you any choice. What can they do? You can see I'm better, can't you?"

"Not really, boss. To be honest I think what just happened in there hasn't done you any favours. Perhaps we should stop in the motorway services and you can see if you can do anything with a bit of makeup to make you look less like the walking dead, ma'am."

They laughed at the final, ironic, address. It was brief but it lightened the mood in the car as they turned for home.

Chapter 60

Tanya wasn't particularly worried as she walked the corridor to Bob Scunthorpe's office. She had disobeyed the medical staff's instructions and if he wanted to give her a bollocking, then so be it. She would show him the progress they'd made and assure him that she felt better. She wasn't sure that it was true, but the headache was held at bay by a mixture of adrenaline and painkillers. For her, the fact that she was still alive, and functioning, was enough at the moment.

What she hadn't expected was to find the Assistant Chief Constable sitting in one of the visitor's chairs, a mug of coffee in his hand. She moved further into the room and Brian Finch nodded at her from the other side of the small coffee table. They were grouped in the area away from the DCI's desk. It had the appearance of a friendly little get together. Her stomach clenched.

Bob Scunthorpe didn't smile at her. This seemed over the top for a minor infraction, unless it was coincidence that the ACC was there. She clutched at the fragile straw.

"You wanted to see me, sir?" she said.

"Yes, come and sit down, Detective Inspector, before you fall down. I think you have already been told that you shouldn't be on duty and looking at you it's pretty obvious why. However, we'll leave that issue until later."

"I'm fine, sir. Well maybe not fine, but I truly believe that I'm well enough to be working."

There was a flash of impatience in his eyes. She held her peace and took a seat on the remaining chair. There was no offer of coffee and the smell of it was torment.

"I'll cut straight to the chase. We've received a complaint and the Assistant Chief Constable has asked that the case you are currently involved in be handed over to Detective Inspector Finch. Please make all the information you have available to him immediately. We will re-assign your team. As it turns out this is probably for the best. You can have a week to recover from your concussion, and then come back ready to take on something else..." Scunthorpe glanced at the solemn looking officer who would not meet Tanya's eyes but stared down at the cup in his hand. Of course 'asked' wasn't the truth of it.

Tanya had never experienced an episode of total speechlessness. She truly could not form words. Brian Finch watched her, smug and amused. At that moment she wanted to lash out, to wipe the expression from his face. She gulped, struggled with the racing thoughts until, after what felt like an age, she finally managed to speak. "If there has been a complaint, sir, shouldn't my union representative be here?"

"We can go that way if you wish, Detective Inspector, but we rather hoped to keep this on a more informal level. That way there will be no need to have a written record, no black marks against anyone." The ACC's voice was low and quiet.

"What complaints have been made, sir? By whom?" Tanya struggled to keep her response measured and respectful, but she seethed with anger. This was wrong. She hadn't done anything that could have been cause for complaint.

"I was contacted by Mrs Patricia Baker. As you know she has recently been widowed under the most distressing circumstances. Her husband, Peter, was a close friend," said the ACC.

"Sir, what is it exactly that Mrs Baker is complaining about? I believe that I was sensitive and considerate when I visited her. The news that her husband's death is now to be treated as suspicious was difficult, I do understand that, but what am I supposed to have done?"

"I think it is enough that Mrs Baker has asked that someone else handle the investigation into her husband's death, and as DI Finch has been involved, we have judged it politic for him to be assigned. Now, if you wish to make a fuss about this, contact your union representative and what have you, then so be it. However, I think we should consider the facts here. You haven't made progress with the original investigation. You have initiated surveillance on a member of the public without following the correct protocol, searched his vehicle without a warrant, and managed to get yourself injured into the bargain. I think, to be honest, Detective Inspector Miller that it would be best for you to step back, absent yourself on sick leave, and allow Detective Inspector Finch to take this forward."

"Sir, I brought Mulholland in, I feel sure that we'll get a conviction." Tanya felt the panic rise. She wasn't sure what she had just said was true but was determined to fight her corner. "If I may…"

The ACC had put his mug on the table and picked up his uniform hat. The rest of them stood as he did, and she was forced into silence.

He was a tall man and bent towards her before he spoke. He invaded her space from above and the action carried a message that was more than just an acknowledgement of their difference in height. "A relatively small case of smuggling and tax avoidance is not very important in the face of what appear to be several murders. It is hardly major crime." The comment was merciless. "I think that's enough. I will leave the details in your hands, Detective Chief Inspector. Now I have another meeting and..." He glanced at his watch. "I'm already late."

As the door closed behind him there was a charged silence. Bob Scunthorpe moved back behind his desk. The cosy little gathering was over, and it was down to business. "I hope you're not intending to make a fuss, Tanya. It can only get messy and you haven't exactly covered yourself in glory."

"Sir, I admit this case has been difficult, progress has been slow. But really, I simply do not see that I did anything that warranted a complaint from Mrs Baker." She hesitated. She needed to tread very carefully now if she was not to sound pathetic and peevish but, although she might be on the canvas, she was not ready to throw in the towel. "If I could have a minute to explain some things, sir?" Bob had always been fair and supportive, and she hoped that, now that the senior officer was gone, he would be more open to listening.

"I made some progress today." She had brought her file with her and held it up now as evidence. "I have names for the body in the shed, and the body in the lake." She glanced at Brian Finch, moved on. "I have a witness. She's being held at Colnburn Detention Centre, but I am going back there tomorrow, and I believe she has information that will move us forward very quickly now." Her mind was racing; how much should she reveal? She could see from his face that what she had said so far hadn't been enough. "About Mrs Baker, sir..." She was aware of Brian Finch glaring at her, huffing now and then, but she blanked him.

"Yes. What about Mrs Baker?" Scunthorpe asked.

She would go for broke. "I have certain concerns regarding her. I had misgivings from the start but it's only since this new information came to light that they have begun to become more... solid."

Brian Finch shifted in his seat, she heard him tut. Ignored it. Bob was waiting but there was interest in his eyes now rather than irritation. She knew he was a believer in gut feeling, in instinct.

"When Mrs Baker was brought from her office, she was told only that there had been an incident involving her husband, and she needed to return to their home. I have checked and confirmed this." Tanya paused again.

She was exhausted. The early start, lack of food and constant reliance on painkillers had made her feel ill and weak. Fleetingly she wondered if it might be the best thing to just walk away and let someone else take over. Then she glanced at the file in her hand, she was all too aware of the photographs they contained. "At no point in our interview with Mrs Baker did she ask what had happened to her husband, what his condition was or indeed where he was."

Brian Finch interrupted. "Oh, for heaven's sake, sir. The woman was in shock, she could see that something serious had happened. This is conjecture and opinion and nothing more."

Bob Scunthorpe held up his hand. "Are you suggesting Mrs Baker had some involvement in the death of her husband, or some foreknowledge?"

"I don't have enough at the moment, but I would like to take it further."

"And this new progress with the other murders? Is it as important as you say, really? Is it enough for me to put my head on the block for?" As Bob Scunthorpe spoke Tanya was aware of Brian Finch shifting to the edge of the chair.

"Sir," he blurted.

Now was the moment to deliver the killer blow, Tanya turned to face Finch. "I was intending to come down to have a word with you, Brian."

Both men waited. "I was able today to help you along with your own case. My witness, Ana, was able to identify the victim that was found in the graveyard. It is a woman known to her." She took a moment to enjoy the building fury evident on his face and flipped open the file. "Emilia, is the name she gave us. She was living in the same place as Ana. When I return tomorrow, I am hopeful I'll be able to obtain more information, something that will lead to you being able to wind your case up.

She was aware she was ignoring the recent discussion and behaving as if she was still in charge of her enquiry. She stopped speaking and waited for Bob Scunthorpe to come to her aid.

Chapter 61

"This puts me in quite a spot here, Detective Inspector," Bob Scunthorpe said.

Brian Finch stood, pushing the chair backwards with the suddenness of the move. "Sir, you can't be serious. I think the ACC was pretty clear. Detective Inspector Miller has not only failed to make progress, but she has antagonised a woman who is just as much a victim as her husband. This vague idea of suspicion falling on Mrs Baker is simply a smoke screen. I really must insist, sir, that we carry out the instruction of the Assistant Chief Constable. I am perfectly able to go to the detention centre myself and question this witness."

"Sir, I don't think that would work. The woman is in a very fragile state. Even with myself and Detective Constable Lewis, she became overwrought and we had to leave because they needed to administer a sedative. A different officer, and especially a male officer is, in my opinion, going to make matters worse and we won't get anywhere," Tanya said.

The DCI steepled his fingers on the desk in front of him. He waited for a moment; the tension was palpable. He lifted his gaze to look directly at Brian Finch. "Thank you for your input, both of you. Brian, I think, as we now have more information, you can leave it to me to speak to the ACC, and we'll discuss these further developments. For the time being, I am allowing Detective Inspector Miller to continue with her investigations. Also, as she has now been able to uncover some helpful information you will probably wish to work with her on the case of the poor young woman who was found in the graveyard. I don't think there is much to be gained at the moment from further discussion. I will be speaking to you both later when I have clarification but, in the meantime, we'll leave things as they are."

There was nothing for them to do now but to leave.

Tanya was the first into the corridor. She nodded at Bob's new secretary as she passed. The thud of Brian Finch's shoes as he rushed to catch up with her made her grin. This was going to be fun.

"Hold on a minute. I need a word."

Tanya stopped and turned, smiled at him. "Why don't we go back to the office. I could do with one of your lovely coffees."

"I haven't got time for that. I'm surprised you have. I want what you have about the victim in my case. Send it to me electronically. And, Tanya..."

She turned to face him full on.

"I expect you think you've been clever, but you'll regret this. I am very interested to know just how you were able to access information about my case, although I have a bloody good idea. I'm going all the way to the top in this job and I will remember this. Oh yes. I will remember this, and you and your spies and toadies will be on my radar," he said.

"I'm sorry, Brian, I can't really send you anything just now. All I have is what the poor woman in detention said." Actually, she had already shared all there was, but she wasn't about to reveal that particular truth. "Soon as I've spoken to her tomorrow I'll be in touch. I think in the meantime it might be useful if you let me have what you have managed to find out so far. If there is anything. You could ask Detective Constable Price to send it on to me if you like."

She turned and left him speechless behind her. She knew she had made an enemy and it was possible that, with his connections, he truly was heading for the top table, but she had bested him. The teams and the DCI would know, and given the grapevine, so would everyone else. She didn't know why it mattered so much, in the face of the greater problems, but it did. It just did.

Chapter 62

By the time she arrived home, Tanya was dead on her feet. She had a drink of milk to wash down more painkillers, a chocolate biscuit, and then staggered upstairs and flopped into bed.

The burble of her mobile phone dragged her out of deep sleep. It was still dark. She hadn't bothered to close the curtains and could see rain blowing against the window; tiny beads lit by the streetlamps raced down the glass. She fumbled for the phone and read Kate Lewis's ID. It was just before seven o'clock.

"Kate. What's happening?"

The other woman didn't bother with apologies for the early hour, or ask whether or not she'd disturbed Tanya, but launched into the drama immediately. "Boss, there's a call from the detention centre. Came through to my mobile for some reason, but I guess it doesn't matter. Ana, the girl we interviewed…" There was a short pause and Tanya could hear Kate breathing rapidly. She heard her take a deep breath. "She's dead, ma'am. That poor, frightened woman is dead."

Tanya had already begun to get up. She had squirmed out from under the duvet to stand shivering in her nightdress, but the shocking words took the strength from her legs; she sat suddenly on the rumpled bed. "I don't understand. What the hell happened?"

She was found in a cleaning cupboard. She'd hung herself, boss. That poor, bloody woman hung herself because of us."

"No, no, just a minute. First of all, how the hell could this have happened? There's going to be hell to pay. And it wasn't because of us, Kate. You can't think like that, you really can't."

"I'm sorry, boss. I just think if we hadn't gone there yesterday, if we hadn't told her about her friends being dead, then she'd still be alive."

"But her friends are dead. Us talking to her didn't change that. Look, where are you?" Tanya could clearly hear her officer sobbing now. "Kate, where are you?"

"I'm in the car, boss. I didn't want to disturb the girls and George."

"Right. I'll meet you at the office. We'll find out just what happened and then…" Tanya's mind was racing, replaying the meeting of the day before – the triumph of getting one up on Brian Finch. "Well, then we have to try and sort out what we do next. Kate, can we try not to let this get out for the moment? Don't tell anyone. If Finch hears about it, we may well lose the case."

"How's that?"

"I need to get dressed and I'll tell you all about it when I see you. Just don't let anyone know what's happened."

"Okay." The detective constable had calmed down now. "Sorry, boss, I didn't ask how you are. I'm sorry I woke you and, for the drama, I should have been able to deal with this better. It just upset me so much."

"I know, Kate, it's ghastly, but we didn't do it. Oh, and I think I'm much better, thank you. I will be when I've nicked coffee from Brian's machine anyway. If you're there before me, get it charged up – yeah?"

"Yes, I will. Sorry, ma'am, I've got myself together now. It was just that I reckon Ana is just a bit older than my eldest and, well…"

"It's okay. I understand. I do."

Chapter 63

Headquarters was still in early morning weekend mode – here and there a few people were using the quiet to catch up on paperwork. There weren't many civilians around – the corridors and most of the offices were dark. Kate had started to make the coffee. She turned as Tanya stepped in. "Boss, I'm sorry for losing it like that."

"It's okay. I realise what a shock it was." Even though she said she understood, Tanya had been surprised. Kate was usually cool under pressure and level-headed. As she handed the cup across the desk the detective constable obviously had more to say.

"I'm all over the place some of the time. I er … I." She paused as her face flushed with embarrassment. "Well to put it bluntly, boss. It's the soddin' menopause. I've had some tests and it's confirmed. I'm now officially an old hag." She tried to laugh but it wasn't convincing.

Tanya didn't know how to react, she remembered her mother complaining about hot flushes, but at the time Tanya had been young – it hadn't meant much to her. That was something that happened to old women. She lowered her eyes to look at the drink in her hand. Kate pressed her lips together. "It makes me a bit illogical at times. I don't quite know how to deal with it yet. I think that had something to do with it, boss. Although I have to say the call was a shock."

"Do you need time off?" It was the only response Tanya could think of. She could see immediately that it had been the wrong one.

Kate shook her head. "It's not like that. This isn't a bout of flu – this is me getting old. No, I don't need time off. I just need to work through it. I'm really sorry about this morning and I'll make sure it doesn't happen again." What might have become a bonding session had ended, and Kate was back to her professional self.

Tanya had never had women friends – not many friends at all come to that – but the ones that she did have were like Charlie Lambert, young cadets, and then newly qualified officers. Fit and young and vigorous. She really didn't know how to handle this. "But you run marathons." It was a stupid comment and Tanya knew it immediately. "Well, you know if you do need some time…" But she could tell it was already over. It was obvious this wasn't something she understood and Kate was no longer a 'could be' friend but back to being just a colleague.

Tanya was glad, relieved. She wasn't good with sympathy and especially with something so obscure.

"No, really, boss, it's fine. If I feel as though things are affecting my work, I'll do something."

This was obviously not the time to mention the tearful phone call again. Tanya pulled the cardboard file from her drawer where it had been locked overnight. "Right, well. There are some things you need to know up front." She spent the next ten minutes relating details of the meeting in Bob Scunthorpe's office.

"So, with this morning's news we are deep in the shit, aren't we? The lead we had, the advantage over Detective Inspector Finch – it's all negated now," Kate said.

"Yes. That's why we've got to keep this quiet for as long as we can. There's no need for the detention centre staff to contact anyone else here. We have to take what we have, which is not much, and try to make some progress with it. I need you on top form, Kate." *Shit, she shouldn't have said that — oh well too late, she couldn't take it back.*

'We'll let Paul Harris know what's happened. Get in touch, will you? We'll have a meeting. Not here, Finch could come in and I don't want to risk it. Let's go back to my house. Send everything you haven't already shared to my computer and then we'll meet Paul back at home."

"It's a bit unusual, ma'am."

"I know and if you're not happy then say so, but I don't see I have any option. Once they know my witness is dead, they could very likely revert to the instructions from the ACC and that's it, I lose the case. I can't let that happen. I especially can't let it happen now. I owe it to them all to find out who has done this, but I owe it even more to poor Ana. Are you with me?"

"Yes, boss."

Chapter 64

They set up a temporary incident room. The images of the whiteboards were displayed electronically on Tanya's sixty-inch screen. Paul Harris drooled when he saw it. It had been a wild extravagance and the truth was she hardly ever used it. Maybe she should think about selling it. Maybe she could sell some of her other stuff, start to reduce her overdraft. She pushed the thoughts aside – now was not the time.

They brought the DS up to date. When he cursed DI Finch, Tanya thought it wasn't the time to remind him of his earlier attempts to befriend the newcomer.

"So, we know she'd been held somewhere and ran away. We know there are other people there, even now, and we know our decapitated victims had also made an escape. It doesn't explain the woman in the graveyard, or why Ana was so convinced that it was her fault she'd been killed." Kate seemed fully in charge again as she went over the facts.

"Are we assuming the bodies had been decapitated and had the hands taken simply to hide their identities?" Paul said.

"As opposed to what?" Tanya asked.

"Well, I don't know. They're foreign, aren't they? Maybe it was some sort of revenge thing, something specific to where they come from. We don't even know for certain where that was yet, do we?"

"I have done some research into the names and they are common in places like Serbia and Bosnia." Kate held up a printed list.

"Well, there we are, those places – they have all sorts of organised crime and what have you," Paul said.

"Oh right, not like here then?" Tanya couldn't help the reaction to his latent racism.

"Well, yeah, but… Oh, it was just a thought."

"Not that helpful really. Can we try and come up with something a bit more useful?"

"Sorry, boss," Harris muttered.

Kate had been reading through the notes and sellotaped the image of Ana to the edge of the giant tv screen. Tanya winced but didn't say anything. The outburst from the officer earlier had made her leery of saying anything that might cause another meltdown.

"I reckon the best lead we have here is Ana. Well, of course it is." Kate corrected herself. "She was the link to all of them and to where the others are kept."

"Do we reckon others are in danger? We don't know how many there are, but it's a few – from the little we were able to find out," Tanya said. "I have to say I'm concerned at the body count since this thing started. Okay, apart from the two original victims, and the graveyard woman, we seem to have had one suicide, Ana. One suicide that has turned out to be murder, and poor old Steven Traynor who seems to be just collateral damage. Though there is a connection between the three foreign victims, how does that connect with Baker… or does it? Maybe that's a different thing, but really what are the chances? And why was Emilia's murder so different?"

"All I will say, ma'am, is that we have to get this bastard. We need to find him, or them, before we have another death." Kate was touching the screen now, one victim image after the other.

Tanya paced the room. "If Ana had no money when she ran away, how did she get to the high street where she was arrested. Did she walk? If she did then we need to start a search around there. I mean, okay, she was young, but how far could she reasonably have walked. She was panicked when she stole the phone because she was desperate to call home, so that indicates to me that it was soon after she had fled."

"She could have hitched though, couldn't she?" Paul said.

"I suppose so, and if she did, that could be helpful if we can find whoever gave her a lift. I would have thought, though, if she did hitch, she would have headed for London – that's where she thought her friends were. And if someone gave her a lift, wouldn't they have let her use their phone? No, I reckon she just walked to the nearest place where she could find a way to call her family. Kate, let's get Google Earth up on the screen." Tanya could feel the buzz of excitement in her belly, she was back on track.

Chapter 65

They peered at the greens, browns and blues of the satellite image. They identified the golf course, the lake known as Duke's Cut. They zoomed closer onto the high street where the drama with the mugging had happened. In and out, close ups of farms and fields pathways and roads. They were not really sure what they were looking for, but just hoping that something would stand out and connect their ideas to things that were fact.

Paul Harris hadn't been at the interview, but he still stared at the screen. "Did she say it was a farmhouse?" he asked.

"An old house and some caravans and a factory."

Tanya pointed at a group of buildings. "What do you think that is?" They all leaned closer.

"Just a farm," Kate said.

"There, what's that one." Tanya pointed at the screen, "I think it's a warehouse or something."

"Hang on I'll zoom in." Kate moved the mouse. "It's industrial for certain and look, there's an old house just a bit away. There looks to be a road connecting them, don't you think?"

"Yeah but what about the caravans?" Harris said.

"Well they're caravans, so they're mobile; perhaps they weren't there then."

"When? How do you mean? Do you reckon they've moved them?"

Kate frowned at him. "No, I don't think so. What I mean is they weren't there at the time this image was taken."

"It's Google Earth. It's a satellite thing isn't it."

The breakdown in communication was irritating Kate. Tanya saw her make fists. She hoped that this was just the stress of this case and not the way that things were going to go; she needed Kate to be her usual cool, efficient self. Maybe she should think again about encouraging her to try for promotion. Then she felt guilty, disloyal to her gender.

The other woman took a breath and obviously calmed herself. "The images are not in real time, Paul. I thought you understood that."

"How do you mean they're not real?"

"They're real, of course they're real, but just not taken now as we're watching. Look." She pointed to the details in the corner of the screen. "There you are this was recorded more than two years ago. In the cities they tend to be more up to date, but in the countryside, though they update them regularly they're not..." She puffed out a sigh. "They're not instant. Look the main thing is that although there are no caravans in the image they could be there now. We have two out of three at this place. I'm going to zoom in, find out where it is and see if there's any more identification. Maybe in street view there'll be a name or something."

They leaned closer, waited for the image to clear as they changed the view. "There..." Tanya was excited as she pointed at the screen. "Can you get closer. Yes, there. It's a factory alright. Woodland or something – is that it?"

Paul read it out loud, trying to regain some kudos. "Yeah, Woodbarn Foods. That name rings a bell. We've heard it recently. That or something very similar. Where the hell was it?"

For a minute no one spoke, and it was Kate who put the thoughts into words. "Oh, bloody hell."

Chapter 66

With the sudden breakthrough, it was difficult not to become over enthusiastic, but Tanya understood that what they really had to do was work deliberately and carefully.

"Kate, go back to the office. Put the facts together so that we can apply for a search warrant. We need to search the factory, the house and anywhere else connected with it. Make it as convincing as you can – everything we have. I'll give you a little while and then call the DCI, alert him to what to expect. Then you send all you have to him. If we can get that sorted, he should be able to justify some more physical help," Tanya said. "Paul, you go and have a look at the house on the ground. You know what you're looking for."

"Yes, boss, the caravans." He glanced at Kate.

"Ideally yes, but anything else of course. You shouldn't really be having to do this on your own, but we have no one else. I'm going to see Mrs Baker. I'm going to try and get access to the factory, better if she takes us in as we won't need a warrant then. It'll be so much quicker. Listen, both of you, we should have backup but there's no one available. We can call in Finch and the other two once we're sure of what we've got, but not yet, not until we have something solid. Take care, keep in touch all the time." She ignored the cynical looks they gave her, knowing that of all of them she had been the guiltiest in recent times of going out on a limb.

She watched them drive away and followed to the junction where Kate turned right to their left. The first thing they had to do was find more proof they were looking at the right location. Acknowledging that she probably was still unfit to drive she was careful. She raised a hand to Paul Harris as he pulled away.

She had to convince Tricia Baker to let her search the factory; she would tell her it was about her husband – it wasn't a lie. For a moment she thought about calling the woman and alerting her to the visit but decided against it.

At the house the big gates were open. The car she recognised as the one at the golf course was parked in front of the garage. She hoped Robin Turner wasn't there, but there was another vehicle in the wide drive. When she saw the white van, Tanya paused; she felt a frisson of excitement. They had looked for a white van from the beginning; they had found one but it had led to nothing except a minor crime. She parked her own car outside, out of sight, and walked back, turned into the drive and went up to the van. She peered through the driver's window, shining the torch on her phone into the dim interior. There were a couple of cans thrown on the floor, a fleecy jacket screwed in a heap on the passenger seat, and on the floor, in the footwell was a black travel bag.

The door was unlocked. She had no search warrant. She glanced around. The garden was empty, but in the house, she could see the glow from the window at the side – the room where she had interviewed Peter Baker and later, his widow. She leaned into the vehicle. There was a piece of plywood screening the rear.

The bag was partly zipped. She took a pair of thin, blue nitrile gloves out of her pocket and pulled them over her fingers. It had begun to rain again, and the damp and her nerves made the task unusually difficult. Once she had her hands covered, she pushed a finger into the gaping top of the holdall, sliding the zipper open. There was a flimsy waterproof jacket on the top; she pulled it out. The front and the sleeves were stained, dark smears and patches, brown against the blue. Under the jacket, there were tools, some of them she recognised, some she did not.

Tanya wanted the bag and even more, she wanted the jacket because she was sure she knew just what the stains were. If anyone found out she had touched them under these circumstances, then they would lose all of their value as evidence. She stuffed the jacket back where she had found it, took a photograph with her mobile phone, moved the zipper back to where she thought it had been and closed the van door. She photographed the number plate and a couple of dents and rust spots on the bodywork. At least they would have some record.

Crouching low against the garden wall she moved to underneath the window of the sun room. Inside she could see Tricia Baker and a bulky, tall man. His hair was shaggy and dark. He was dressed in jeans and a short leather jacket. They were facing each other across the small table. Tricia Baker wagged a finger at him, but he was not cowed and as she watched, Tanya saw him sneer and shake his head.

She crawled nearer. Their voices were raised in anger.

"You have to get rid of them all. Just do it, this has all gone wrong and I'm not carrying the can for you. This was never what we agreed," Tricia Baker shrieked. "None of this was what we agreed. I know what you've done, I know all of it and I will drop you in it without a moment's hesitation. You're a monster. Peter was right about you; he saw what you'd done to that poor man. How could you do that? You're an animal. I should have listened, but I couldn't believe it."

Tanya heard the woman begin to sob. "Now get out of my house and get rid of them all. Today – tomorrow at the latest. I want this over with. I demand that you make this all go away."

"Is not possible. You know is not possible. You think I just wave bye bye, and off they go. No, is not easy. I have to make them listen. I have to show them what will happen if they talk. Why they must not mention my name. I have to make them fear me, show them how long is my reach. It will take about two weeks and then they will be gone, and also, I will be gone. And you..." He paused and leaned closer, his voice a low growl so that Tanya couldn't make out the words. He turned away as he finished speaking and walked towards the door.

"No," Tricia shrieked, "no, that's not good enough. Bogdan, if you don't get them out of here in the next couple of days then I'm going to the police. I'll tell them you threatened me, tell them that you threatened my husband. They'll be interested then; they already know he didn't kill himself. I'll tell them everything. Get my place clear of your strays and weirdos in the next two days or I'm going to the police."

He strode back across the room and reached out to grab Tricia by the hair. Her knees bent as he pulled her head backwards. He leaned towards her, speaking low and urgent in her ears. Again, Tanya couldn't hear what he was saying. She turned to run for the front of the house, she had to get in there before there was yet another casualty. Her feet went from under her, slipping on the wet gravel, and she slid onto the flower border at the side of the drive. As she tried to stand, her feet caught in the tangled branches of a ground-covering shrub. She fell again, rolling in the wet earth under the dripping plantings. Cursing quietly, she scrambled back to her feet and staggered forward.

She reached the corner as the front door smashed back against its hinges and the big man strode down the steps, dragging Tricia Baker with him. She squirmed and struggled in his grip, but she was no match for him.

Tanya's handbag was in the car, her PAVA spray was in there, along with the expandable baton, always kept in the passenger footwell. She had nothing to protect herself, or to help the other woman.

If she revealed herself, if she called out or maybe even rushed him, it might distract the thug, but that would be all. She didn't think she could beat him in a physical fight, normally perhaps, but she was ill and weakened. She drew in a deep breath, ready to yell at him to stop because she couldn't just watch and do nothing. Then she stopped. He could be armed – she remembered the bullet hole in the chest of the dead girl in the lake. This wasn't just her, there was another soul at risk and given his size and obvious anger, the odds were against her.

She needed backup.

She crouched against the wall in the shadows as he opened the rear doors of the van and pushed the screaming Tricia Baker inside. Then, as he pulled away and turned out of the drive, she ran to her car.

As she pulled into the road, her eyes were fixed on his rear lights glowing through the drizzle, one was faulty. She pushed her hand into her pocket for her phone, then the other pocket. She scrabbled on the seat, kicked her feet around the footwell. There was no phone. She remembered the fall, the roll on the sopping ground, and she thumped her hands against the steering wheel in anger and frustration.

Chapter 67

As she followed the white van along the darkening roads, Tanya's mind raced. She struggled to recall the images viewed on Google Earth. If the man called Bogdan was heading for the factory, then Paul Harris was near there. He was driving a pool car which would have a radio, they could call for help. If he wasn't heading there, her situation was pretty dire.

She didn't recognise any of the roads, but it was obvious they were heading out of the built-up area. She muttered pleas under her breath. She had twisted her ankle when she fell, adrenaline had hidden the pain until now. The dull throbbing grew with every movement of her foot. Sharp shards of pain shot through her leg. It wouldn't have to matter. When they got wherever he was leading, she would have to act; somehow, she had to act.

The streetlamps had ended some time ago and there was the risk he would see her headlights and suspect she was following him. The roads were empty on what was a wet and inhospitable Sunday evening; just the two of them rushing through the landscape. But then, why should he be worried? He didn't know she had been at the house. In any case, there was no choice. She couldn't risk letting him pull too far ahead, she couldn't lose him.

She was still unsure about just where they were, and the geography of the area was not clear in her mind. There were large houses set back from the roads, long drives, and floodlighting. Now and then they passed smaller cottages and she could see farm buildings but nowhere were there factories that she recognised.

Then he began to slow. She pulled back further. He didn't indicate – why should he on this deserted stretch of highway? – but she watched as the van turned into a side road. She drove past the junction. If he had been aware of her then it would reassure him, but it gave her a chance to glance down the narrow road which was illuminated by his headlights. In front of him was a wire fence and a pair of gates, beyond that was the dark shape of a large building. The wooden sign they had been able to read on the Google street view was unreadable but recognisable. He had come to the factory.

She should try to find Paul Harris but it was difficult to relate the view they had seen on the computer with these real roads in the dark. She could drive around until she maybe found the road leading to the house and hopefully the caravans. But then, she wasn't certain this was even the right place. Or she could just drive down to the factory and hope that there would be a way to bring Tricia Baker out of danger. Then she could call for the back-up she would need to arrest Bogdan. At the very least she could take the woman to safety.

She peered around her, visibility was awful, and she assumed that Paul Harris would have had the sense to hide his car from anyone at the farm, so it would be hidden from her as well. There really was no other option, no time to waste. She turned down the narrow road and pulled across the front of the gates. If he tried to drive away, she had at least sealed off one means of escape. Of course, there could be others. She grabbed her PAVA spray can and her night stick and stepped out into the darkness. As her foot hit the floor she gasped with the pain in her ankle, hopped forward a couple of steps and then forced herself to walk, pushing through the pain.

Chapter 68

He had unlocked the gates and then pushed them together after driving through. A heavy chain and padlock dangled loose. Tanya pushed them open just enough to slide between and then closed the gap behind her, wrapping the chain between the bars. Block off any mean of escape – it was rudimentary training.

The building was a huge metal shed. There was a nasty smell in the air and as she drew nearer it caused her to alter her breathing. There were huge bins ranged beside the walls and the stink was unspeakable. The stench was of death, so she had to look. On the floor beside one of the bins was a dark object, her eyes were drawn to the chicken's head, small and pathetic in the falling rain. She lifted the lid; feet and heads and innards were piled inside in ghastly heaps. She recoiled but it was too late to stop the revulsion in her stomach and she bent with her hand against the cold wall, retching and coughing.

There were many dark piles of equipment, pallets and boxes, the things that you would expect around an industrial unit and she moved through them. Behind the first building was a second one. Faint light leaked from around the doorways and beneath the roof. From inside there was the sound of life in the quiet of the night.

Towards the rear of the larger building, metal steps led to a door on an upper floor and beside that was a window. Harsh, white light gleamed through the rain and out across the fields. It might be a security office but the fact that Bogdan had brought Tricia Baker here made it unlikely, so it was probable she had found them.

In the shadow of the building, she walked towards the stairs. There was no plan in her mind. He was a powerful looking individual, he could be armed with a gun. He probably wouldn't need a weapon to overpower her and there was little to no chance of Tricia Baker being much help. Still, duty pushed her on. There was no way the body count was going to increase if there was the slightest chance that she could stop it.

Her soft trainers made scuffling noises on the metal steps and, reaching the narrow landing, she crouched below the window. Her throat was dry, the headache had returned, and her ankle was on fire. Tanya lowered her head for just a moment and wiped a sleeve across her rain-drenched face.

Slowly and carefully she unbent enough to see. He was in there. Tricia Baker was slumped on a black leather chair, her face tear-stained and terrified. Bogdan was sitting on the edge of the desk holding a gun in his hand. Tanya didn't have enough knowledge to identify it and the type of weapon was meaningless anyway. It would be enough to do terrible damage to a soft human body; it could very well be the one that had already killed. She felt her stomach turn but drove back the fear – there was really no option, she would need to do something.

She leaned to the door and slowly pushed down on the metal handle. She heard the click of the lock, loud in the night. She pushed, just enough to move the latch across the strike plate. She took a deep breath, uncurled to her full height and with the night stick in one hand, her can of spray held before her, she kicked at the door. It flew back bouncing off the interior wall with a rattling thud and the two people in the room spun around towards her. Tricia Baker screamed as Bogdan raised the weapon and the roar of gunfire filled the small office.

Chapter 69

Tanya flung herself to the ground as she burst through the door and the bullet flew harmlessly into the night. Later she would wonder where it had ended up, but right then she was scrabbling to stand, flailing with her stick. It connected with Bogdan's powerful shoulders, but he shrugged off the assault. She pulled back again and aimed for his hand already raised, ready to shoot a second time. She was aware of Tricia screeching in the background and the yelling from the thug, but it was peripheral – all her effort was concentrated on the weapon and her feeble chance to disarm him.

She brought the stick down with all the power she could manage. As she did, she sprayed the can into his face with the other hand. The angry roaring changed to a yell of shock and pain and she swiped, downwards and sideways with the baton. The gun flew from his grasp to skitter across the floor. She moved nearer, still spraying. He lashed out blindly, knocking the PAVA from her hand. He drew back his arm and, moving instinctively, he punched towards where he thought she was. She swivelled away, and the blow landed against her shoulder. She grunted with pain but did not fall. She raised her stick one more time and lashed it sideways across his face. The yell this time was louder, more of a shriek, and he covered his eyes with both hands. She pressed on, striking again at the side of his head.

He fell to the floor and it seemed she had him, but he rolled over, stretching to sweep the floor with both hands. When he pushed to his knees, he held the gun. He was facing away from Tanya now, waving the gun blindly in front of him and Tricia Baker was directly in his line of fire. As she saw his finger move on the trigger guard Tanya yelled out, raised the baton and brought it down hard on his wrist. The gun barked loud into the night, but the bullet this time hit the wall. He was still not disarmed.

She dropped the stick, grabbed his hand with both of hers and bent backwards, sharp and sudden, as hard as she was able, every bit of her strength concentrated on that one action. He screamed again as the gun hit the floor and she kicked it aside. Bogdan was bent forward now, groaning and holding his broken wrist. Tricia Baker fell from the chair and grabbed the weapon. She backed against the wall and stood in terrified silence, tears streaking down her face, the gun held in both shaking hands in front of her.

Tanya glanced back and forth between them. She closed her eyes for a fleeting moment and then, in desperation, spun towards Bogdan. Two steps forward and then with as much power as she could summon, she brought her knee up into his groin and watched as he crumbled to a gasping, retching heap on the office floor. Before there was chance for him to recover, she grabbed his arms. The crepitation as she moved the damaged wrist, bone on bone, made her nauseous, but she dragged his hands behind his back and around the leg of the heavy metal desk. Pulling handcuffs from her jeans pocket she snapped them over the thick and swelling wrists.

After a second to catch her breath she stood to face the other woman who was sobbing now, the gun lowered in front of her but still gripped in both hands.

"Give me that, Mrs Baker. You don't need it now. Just give it to me." Tanya reached out and pried the weapon away. "I need your phone."

The woman stared at her uncomprehending for a moment. "He killed my husband. Poor Peter, he was so badly shaken when he found the body at the golf course. Then when he saw the image of the other one, the girl, he knew. He'd seen her at the factory. I told him not to look at the papers but he couldn't help himself. He confronted Bogdan and told him to leave. He should never have done that. He was so very frightened that he wouldn't come back to work. He wanted us to run away. But I couldn't, you see that don't you," she said.

"When they came for me, to bring me home." Her tears were flowing freely now.

Although she needed to call for help, Tanya didn't want to interrupt. She let her speak.

"I knew. I knew something awful had happened. I thought it was true when they said that he killed himself. I felt so guilty. Then when you came and said he was murdered. Well, it was obvious, wasn't it? I didn't know what to do," Tricia continued.

She reached and grasped hold of Tanya's arm, the thin fingers claw-like where they dug into soft flesh. "I told him he had to go. I cancelled the staffing contract with him. He mocked me, told me how he'd done it. Replayed it for me, said that I would be next. Poor Peter, he must have been so very frightened. I've been scared, and today I was going to run, but he came to the house."

She looked down at the man on the floor, his eyes glazed with pain, and she spat at him. "You're nothing more than an animal – vile and brutal. I rue the day I ever heard of you." With that final word, she slid to the floor and curled her knees up towards her chest and sobbed.

Tanya knelt in front of her. "I need your phone, Tricia."

She seemed to come out of the fugue; she shook her head. "No, I don't have my phone. There!" She pointed to the desk and the landline on the top of it.

Chapter 70

It was a multi-departmental operation to sort out the backlash. Paul Harris had found the farm, and when he saw just what faced him, he tried to call Tanya. He had peered through the farmhouse windows, saw movement in the gloomy interior. He knocked on the door, but they were locked inside – frightened and confused individuals on thin, filthy mattresses; a number of young women locked in old, dilapidated caravans, the toilets draining into holes in the ground underneath. The ghastliness of it overwhelmed him.

There had been no answer to his call. So, he called Kate for advice. She swung into action. A phalanx of uniformed officers, the social services, immigration authorities and an expanded investigation team, including Sue Rollinson, Dan Price and a seething and disgruntled Brian Finch were drafted in to help.

The pathetic slaves rescued from the damp and dirty farmhouse and the small cluster of caravans, were mostly admitted to hospital in the first instance. Over the following weeks, some returned home, their expenses paid by their embassies. They were heartbroken with disappointment, their hopes of a better future shattered.

Some were taken into the social care system. Their mental health was too fragile for anything more than care for the foreseeable future.

There was one young man, Pietre who had been badly beaten and it was days before they were able to talk to him. If Paul Harris hadn't found him when he did, then the chances were that he would have added to the unacceptably long list of the dead. It was he, through an interpreter who told them about Emilia, and Bogdan's fury when he found Ana had escaped.

"He hit her so much. He didn't believe her when she told him that she had been asleep." The young man said. "He beat her and beat her. I was outside. I cannot sleep in the house with all the men snoring; and the smell is bad. When they are all asleep, I have found a way through the cellar. I can be in the field, secret and quiet so they do not see. I tried to help her but, three of them beat her. They beat me also and I thought I would die. I didn't, but Emilia, I think she did. I saw them put her in the back of the white van."

There was plenty of evidence in the back of the VW to prove what he said to be true. There was DNA to link the vehicle to all three deaths. There were also fingerprints on the glass from the kitchen at Baker's house. Two men who were living in another, much better mobile home, tried to run when the noise woke them but were stopped on the road and brought back.

When they were questioned later, they refused to speak except to demand help from their embassy. It was going to be a long time before everything was sorted and all the threads pulled together. The team agreed that when it was time for the bodies to be released, they would all go together to the airport to witness the sad repatriation, but that was for later. Elian, the man from the hut, would be returned to his home in no fit state to be seen by his loved ones, his skull still missing in the wild.

It was unclear just how much Patricia Baker had known. Her brother was her legal representative and forbade her to answer any of their questions. She did, however, reiterate that she believed Bogdan had killed her husband. "We weren't that close anymore. Me and Peter. Well, we'd been married a long time, you know. There was no romance or anything like that. We rubbed along though, the two of us. I miss him. I really miss him."

In the end, the CPS decided there wasn't enough evidence to charge her with anything. Yes, the factory had been staffed with Eastern Europeans but there was no crime there, and they couldn't prove she knew the circumstances they were being kept in. "Bogdan rented the farmhouse from us," she told them, "I knew there were caravans. But I never went there. Why would I go there? It was nothing to do with me," she said. It was another factor in the whole situation that made Tanya despair of her fellow citizens.

Chapter 71

Bob Scunthorpe was effusive in his praise of Tanya and her little team. "You need to take some time off, Inspector. Take a week's sick leave. I'm sure if we need your input we know where to find you."

Of course, she declined, she needed to see it through to the end. Bogdan and his cohorts were remanded in custody and the slow wheels of justice had begun to grind forward.

They dotted all the i's that they could, piecing together evidence from the other workers. Brian Finch stalked the offices in quiet fury. His case became part of the whole, so his thunder was not only stolen, it was as if it had never existed as a separate entity.

The day that the paperwork was finally finished, and the whiteboards cleared, Tanya was sent for by the DCI. It was *déjà vu* when she walked into the office to find the ACC and Brian Finch already there.

"Coffee, Detective Inspector?" Bob smiled at her. She was almost back to normal and was surprised to find that she was looking forward to the drinks in the pub planned for later. "The Assistant Chief Constable wanted to add his congratulations to mine, and he has some news."

She had been put forward for a commendation. Her bravery in rescuing Patricia Baker and arresting an armed thug on her own, would be officially recognised.

"I was particularly impressed, Detective Inspector, that you refused to be dissuaded when you were convinced that you were on the right track. What is it they say nowadays – 'speaking truth to power'? Well done." Tanya was speechless; it seemed to be becoming a habit.

She glanced at Brian Finch who had been a silent and brooding presence. Bob Scunthorpe noticed; he cleared his throat. "There is just one other thing, we thought it right that you be the first to know."

Brian looked up and grinned at her. She felt the first stirrings of alarm. Bob Scunthorpe continued. "Brian's next posting has been delayed." He glanced at Finch. "So, for the foreseeable future, the current situation will continue. I trust that you'll be able to see past the recent… awkwardness. I'm sure you will. You are both highly professional officers."

The satisfaction of the ACC's congratulations, the pride in the commendation, even the anticipation of the pub, faded to grey.

$$* * *$$

In the incident room, Finch told them all the news. "So, we are going to be working together for a good while longer." Sue Rollinson was positively glowing, and Tanya wondered how well they had actually got on. There had been no rumour that she was aware of. However, she had been preoccupied.

Kate was looking across the room. When Tanya caught her eye, she grimaced but followed it with a quick wink. Tanya smiled back.

She pushed the irritation to one side and enjoyed the evening in the pub. Just a bit drunk – tired but satisfied – she took a taxi home.

She wanted to call Charlie; he'd been there at the last gathering. Every time she had looked at Finch, she missed Charlie just a bit more. But it was too late, she couldn't risk waking the baby. She'd call him the next day and have a good old moan about the unfairness of it all.

She picked up the mail that had been gathering on the hall table over the last few days. Plenty of catalogues: Sweaty Betty, Boden, Hobbs – all the usual suspects. She put them to one side.

There were three from the bank. She gritted her teeth – they wouldn't be cheerful. It was a long time since she'd opened bank correspondence happily. Yes, they were worse than she thought. She had exceeded her overdraft by quite a bit. They were threatening her credit cards. She walked into the living room and stared at the wall for a minute and then she sent Paul Harris a text.

If you want to buy that screen make me an offer. :-)

She wouldn't miss it, although it would hardly make a dent in the debt. She'd have to do more. Some of her clothes would need to go on eBay.

There was one more envelope. It was a letter from Serena. That in itself was odd, an email would have been more usual. In the event, it was rather lovely. It thanked her, apologised for the trouble she'd caused, brought her up to date on the ongoing turmoil in Edinburgh: her sister's divorce, the wrangling about the house, and finally a request that they keep in touch. She folded it back into the envelope. Did she really want that? She didn't know.

Did she want Kate as a friend? Kate with her developing problems and the way that they made her face the passing of her own years?

Then there was Simon – she still hadn't got back to him about 'the date'. She looked around the quiet room. Wasn't this enough for her? This, the occasional chat with Charlie, and her job. Most of all her job.

She passed Serena's letter through the shredder, poured herself a hefty glass of whisky and dialled Simon Hewitt on her mobile

The End

List of characters

The Team:

Robert (Bob) Scunthorpe – Detective Chief Inspector

Late fifties. Decent and honourable senior officer. Married.
One son.

Tanya Miller – Detective Inspector

Early thirties. Younger daughter in the family with one
sibling. Always in the shadow of her brilliant older sister as
they grew up. A shopaholic, she returned to Oxford from
a previous posting and at first worked in the missing
persons section until moving to the serious crimes team.

Sue Rollinson – Detective Constable

Suhita Rollinson-Bahkshi. Young, unmarried, from a
largish mixed-race family, father dead, mother an estate
agent. Three brothers one sister.

Paul Harris – Detective Sergeant

A plodder. Recently married and a bit of a bloke. Doesn't really get the whole PC thing. Lives in a rental flat with his wife Nicole.

Kate Lewis – Detective Constable

Fifty, heading for retirement. Content with her life and achievements but refuses to be side-lined due to her age and lack of professional progression. Happily married with three teenaged daughters. Skilled with the computer and a good organiser. Husband called George.

Dan Price – Detective Constable

Young and insecure. Quiet and keeps his head down. Partly because he was bullied when he was younger but also because he isn't sure how widely known it is that he is gay. Lives at home with his parents and one kid sister who is still at school.

Charlie Lambert – Detective Inspector

Recently moved to Merseyside. Married to Carol. They have one baby – Joshua – whom he dotes on. He is a family man from a large Jamaican family.

Brian Finch

New DI – tall, good looking, computer savvy and connected via an uncle to the top brass. Arrogant and driven.

Simon Hewitt – medical examiner

Tall, good looking, dark brown hair and grey eyes, late forties, unmarried.

Moira – receptionist at the morgue

Late thirties and dedicated to 'protecting' the morgue staff from hassle. Abrupt and unfriendly but tolerated by the morgue staff as she runs the place so efficiently.

Lisa Cummings – medical examiner; newly qualified

Thirty, married with one child.

Karen Laidlaw – PCSO

Newly qualified, kind and dedicated.

The public at the Oxford Links Golf Club:

Spencer Cartwright – witness

Peter Baker – witness

Bob Peters – witness

Steven Traynor – club secretary

Jamie Mulholland – bar manager

Tricia Baker (Patricia) – married to Peter Baker

Robin Turner, her brother – a solicitor

If you enjoyed this book, please let others know by leaving a quick review on Amazon. Also, if you spot anything untoward in the paperback, get in touch. We strive for the best quality and appreciate reader feedback.

editor@thebookfolks.com

www.thebookfolks.com

Other books by Diane Dickson

In this series:

BROKEN ANGEL (Book 1)
BURNING GREED (Book 2)
BRAZEN ESCAPE (Book 4)
BLURRED LINES (Book 5)

The DI Jordan Carr Series:

BODY ON THE SHORE
BODY BY THE DOCKS
BODY OUT OF PLACE
BODY IN THE SQUAT
BODY IN THE CANAL
BODY ON THE ESTATE
BODY BELOW THE BRIDGE
BODY IN THE WAY

Others:

TWIST OF TRUTH
TANGLED TRUTH
BONE BABY
LEAVING GEORGE
WHO FOLLOWS
THE GRAVE
PICTURES OF YOU
LAYERS OF LIES
DEPTHS OF DECEPTION
YOU'RE DEAD
SINGLE TO EDINBURGH
HOPELESS